# Sea of

# Movement

Written by: Jeff Kozlowski

Sea of Movement

Lulu.com
Publish and Sell Worldwide


For more information contact Jeff Kozlowski:

jeffreykozlowski@yahoo.com
www.myspace.com/jeffkozlowski


ISBN 978-1-4303-2703-5
Printed in the United States of America

*Sea of Movement* is dedicated to
my wife Kari, daughter Kana, and
son Kellen for their love of life and the
endless moments of joy they give me.

## ACKNOWLEDGEMENTS:

I want to thank the surfers I know who enjoy a great surf session as much as I do. I hope this story captures the essence of our fleeting moments of connection to the sea.

I'd also like to thank the readers of my first two chapters in the First Chapters contest for your invaluable input. The constructive feedback I received helped give this story the life it truly deserves.

A warm thanks goes to the friends I have connected with online. You have often moved me with your personal stories, poems, and words of encouragement. I never imagined that writing would lead me to such a great group of people.

I want to thank my wife for believing in me and supporting my love of writing even when I felt like I couldn't write another word. Somehow you always help me move forward and onto the next page. You know that the experience of meeting you on Maui helped create the concept for this novel.

I want to thank my children for understanding why I'm always in front of my computer in between baseball practice and dance lessons. I can't wait to share this story with the two of you someday.

A special thanks goes to Jack Johnson for his thought provoking melodies. Your songs continuously played in the background as I wrote about my characters' lives, struggles, and realizations. It's *your* natural gift of music that inspired me to create a character as rich in depth and talent as Nathan Jansen.

Finally, to all of my readers, thank you for your continued support. I hope you enjoy reading *Sea of Movement*.

## Prologue

*Nikki Thomsen paused along the same Bengali pathway she'd walked countless times in 1991, anticipating the return of the man who'd caused her so much pleasure and pain. It had been nearly three years since her life had collapsed, and it had taken her that long to prepare for this chance at redemption. While making her way down to the ocean, she noticed how the blond beaches and dense foliage had so fully recovered, and began to hum a familiar tune. But waves of nostalgia and grief returned from scarred depths; phantoms of tragedy lingered in the breeze. She squeezed the small wooden chest in her arms, hoping its contents would grant a chance at fulfillment.*

*Nikki's most vivid memory was the time just after the storm, when she'd fallen into a morning ritual of walking down the coast to lament the piles of dead bodies littering the beach. Staring now at a dried streambed, she remembered the spot where stacks of rotting cattle had created a bronzed waterfall, temporarily damning the putrid water that seeped back into the ocean. Rigor mortise had set in and two of the cows' stiffened legs met to form a bony cross. Unable to admit that she was shattered from the nauseating stench of human and animal flesh mixing with the depth of her emotions, she sought comfort in the remains. In fact, she considered the body parts a temple of remorse, her direct connection to the lost souls. Each day, she would talk and sing to the thousands of bewildered spirits of Bangladesh, as it was her only means of healing.*

*Of course, that twisted symbol was gone now, nothing more than a charred image tucked away in the unconscious. The catastrophe had quenched her naïveté, ripping apart her optimistic perception and convincing her of the truth. It had taken years of desperate suffering to accept the genuine nature of her purpose. Only after letting go of the fear and accepting her fate did she realize that creating real change requires unanticipated tears, life-altering sacrifice, and inevitable loss.*

*She'd learned how to move forward by locking the suffering inside the hopes and dreams of the missing chest. Now, two weeks had passed since her folks received a knock on their door from an Indonesian fisherman. He claimed he'd found the half-buried remnants of a raft just west of his ocean side home. When Nikki's parents called with the news of her recovered property, she knew the time had come to begin the next phase of her search.*

*Indeed, the contents of the trunk contained a raw record of that time, a tender elegy grieving their lost way of life. And the optimism within that message could make things right in her tainted world.*

*She searched the sky for the plane that held the key to a brighter future. There was no turning back.*

## 1.

A fiery dusk faded to glowing embers as Nikki Thomsen came riding upon the circle of wave-worn surfers. Her spotted mare, Yonkers, stepped carefully through the on-lookers and faced the carefree musicians lounging by the evening fire. While taking in the scene, the young woman intuitively knew she was in for days of pleasure, discovery, and adventure.

Four of the sun-baked young men were staring into the flames to keep together in their spontaneous live performance, although one of them was nearly passed out from too much wine. The fun-loving Billy Windsor had a gleeful smile on his face as he played his ukulele, strumming the same three chords in a series of variations. Wiry-haired and dread-locked Garo Bohio, a Caribbean drifter who could play any instrument without lesson, set the tempo on the tribal drum he'd picked up in the Solomon islands, while the clowning Charlie 'Charge' Dunley tapped sporadically on a wooden xylophone, demonstrating a hint of rhythm despite his inebriated state.

In the center, Nathan Jansen was lost in the soft vocals he was making up on the spot, reworking lyrics from a song about surfing the night sky. When he let out three consecutive lines about dropping in on the Milky Way, his spectators' thoughts turned towards the heavens and he felt he might be on to something special.

For the previous fifteen months, the core group had searched for seamless waves through much of South America, across the east coast of Australia, and among dozens of islands tucked away in the South Pacific. The past month was spent following the swells along the North Island of New Zealand. Each discovery was like a Garden of Eden, divine settings tempting them with brilliance, whether they were snowy backdrops rising above the horizon or lush overhangs jutting into the turquoise sea. Larger-than-life stories of sessions at

Desperations, Papamoa, Sateva Suckbowl, Coloseums, and Raglan outranked memories of extreme rides from previous adventures. But for the guys, it wasn't about showboating in front of friends or bragging about rides to local children hanging around the campsite.

What it was really about was breaking away, developing out-and-out freedom, entering a world few dared explore. It was about the brief connection with source, a sweeping dance with Mother Nature, a fleeting frolic with her power. And one could only find that kind of peace from within. When the sun goes down and the crowd heads home, only the individual soul can comprehend the fulfillment of the untamed interaction between man and wave. And that's why Billy had taken them on this trip, not to gain status, but to discover purpose in the human pursuit for perfection.

Billy's yacht, appropriately named *Rumrunner*, was anchored just off a deserted beach south of Anawhata. The crew had stayed there for the better part of three days because a swell had produced hollow tubes to the north of the giant rocky island dividing the beach. For the guys, this was the latest highlight in a fantasy trip that was topped everyday. For Nikki Thomsen, it was simply home.

From her mount, she got her first good look at the four men. They were living the life she desired and she hoped she'd become a part of it all. Nathan Jansen, his broad shoulders shadowing the firelight as he strummed his guitar, stood out to her at once. Pausing to watch him sing, she was impressed with his boyish features, the soft curve in his lips and the deep passion in his eyes.

The fire cracked; the guys looked up at the same moment and stopped playing as they noticed Yonkers' nostrils flaring and Nikki's hazel eyes glaring at them from above the skyline. Nathan's voice trailed awkwardly into the passing wind and everyone had a laugh when he gasped at her natural beauty. She saw that he was different than the rest, softer spoken and better mannered, maybe the man she'd been waiting for.

She spoke from her mount. "G'evening boys, hate to break up your party, but my pop asked me to see you off."

Billy grinned at her and asked, "And who might you be?"

"My name's Nikki and up there, beyond that bluff, that's my parent's land."

He joked back, "Well, how about you join us so we can we stay awhile longer?"

Having gained their full attention through her family's standing, she spoke in a pleasant tone. "My pop would've preferred to make himself known, but I had to come see this for myself. I've been listening to you boys from up on the knoll for the past hour." She looked at Nathan and continued, "And I have to tell you mate, you've the loveliest singing voice I've ever heard."

Her gentle ambiance had swallowed him whole. Nathan wouldn't have been more captivated if a divine enchantress had come drifting in on a jeweled vessel from beyond the horizon. He believed he had found perfection a few times in the crest of a wave, but in front of him was a woman who made him shudder. The focus of her compliment filled him with uneasiness and he was unable to respond other than to give a shy smile.

Billy answered for his friend with a cocky wisecrack, "Yah, he calls them in with that sweet voice of his and they come a' flockin' to me."

Noticing two beautiful young women on either side of him, Nikki answered with a stitch of sarcasm. "I wonder what you'd do without him then?"

He smirked and shot back, "I'd probably be chasing after you instead of waiting for you to come find me."

She glanced again at Nathan and replied, "He's a bit of a cocky dag, now isn't he?" Yet, Nikki couldn't help but notice Billy Windsor's handsome features, those high cheekbones, his classic nose. She was drawn to his high-spirited demeanor and larger than life personality. Immediately, she picked up on his social status because she had attracted men of a similar air. Above all, she knew he was the leader of the group, a bad boy with all the answers, which was a perfect reason to avoid him.

Garo continued to tap his drums, but the rest of the guys were forced to take a break from their jam session because Charge's head was nodding off between his knees, a full beer spilling in the sand beside him. Nikki jumped down off of Yonkers, tied her to a large piece of driftwood, and asked Nathan to make room for her beside the fire. From the moment she sat down, there wasn't another living soul around as far as Nathan was concerned. In her lighthearted tone, she asked, "So what brings you around these glorious parts?"

"We found some nice waves to surf a few days back and can't bring ourselves to leave."

"Oh, so you're a surfer, are you? Good on ya, mate." Then, laughing, she said, "I bet you're a mad sook out there with the steep breaks we've been having."

Unsure what she'd called him, he replied, "I just try to keep up with the rest of the guys that's all."

"Like your friend over there?"

"Billy? Yah, he's alright."

She nodded over at Billy and asked, "So are all of you bludging off him or are you independently wealthy as well?" Nathan blushed. She was quite forward in her line of questioning, conveying the fact that she was familiar with the privileged class. But she didn't flaunt her status; in fact, her demeanor made it clear that she had seen her share of demons.

Keeping it light, she asked, "Would you happen to have a drink to share with a fine young lady such as myself?"

"Sure. What would you like?"

"Oh, just grab me a stubby out'a the chilly bin. Unless you can pour me a shandy of course."

"How do I make that?"

Nikki laughed and said, "No worries. A beer'd be nice, me Luv."

Enamored by her accent, he nodded and said, "Great, then you'll stay awhile." He turned to reach into the cooler and caught a glimpse of her long black hair outlining the curves of her body. He knew this was an opportunity to move forward from the pain, to begin letting go of the indolence that had been packaged by his family as a stable life and successful future. Putting it all on the line,

11

he asked, "It's a beautiful night, would you like to take a walk along the beach?"

He knew he'd take some heat from his friends for the ineptness of his game, the breakup leaving his charisma skinned with vulnerability. But he was shocked when he heard her reply, "Sounds delightful. How 'bout I show you around the bluffs. Maybe take in a bit of mum's riding land."

With his heart pounding, he replied, "I'd like that. Lead the way."

There were some catcalls as she got up, untied the horse, and led him to the silver strip of the beach trail. Soon they were walking side by side up a sloped dune, keeping pace with Yonkers' soft hoofs clopping in the sand. The intricacies of the group's lifestyle had become clear to Nikki the moment she'd heard their music. She knew the guys had perfected their version of the American dream. But as she looked Nathan over, she concluded that he didn't fit in with the rest. She asked, "So, why are you half way around the world?"

He looked embarrassed and said, "In between my parent's dreams, I needed to take some time for myself."

"How sad."

He wanted to spill his guts and tell her about the pressures his family had put on him to succeed. The business major his mom had chosen for him, the practically arranged engagement to Tamara, the plan for partnership with his step-dad, so many factors driving him to escape, forcing him to make a run at his dream before settling for the *comfortable* life. Yet he didn't want to scare her away with

12

stories of his misery back home. Besides, since his breakout, he had cherished every moment of the experience as if it were a gift from Lono, the Hawaiian god of prosperity.

So he described the fantasy to her, how they'd wake up every morning before dawn to search for waves, leaving the captain and crew in charge of the ship as they set out on the Zodiac exploring every corner of a new paradise. Each day was a different adventure and getting sidetracked was part of the fun. Sometimes they'd take a morning dip in giant tide pools to loosen up the hangover or speed up a narrow inlet while towing each other on rigged boards. Once in a while they'd happen upon local villagers drifting by on a flatboat and attempt a gestured conversation. He could have gone on all night about their journeys, but realized he was controlling the conversation.

Nikki saw his glossy eyes and stopped him mid-sentence. She was half joking when she said, "Sounds more like an addiction than an adventure."

"Well, you're right. As much fun as it is, I sometimes go off by myself in the smaller Zodiac to spend the morning exploring sea caves or checking out the wildlife. The guys are great and all, but I need time alone to energize myself."

"So what do you do to fill the void?"

"What do you mean?" There were countless activities to fill the void, ocean pastimes like scuba diving, spear fishing, cliff diving, or jet skiing. Not to mention good ole' fashion fun like playing volleyball on the deck, engaging in chicken fights in the pool, pulling practical jokes, making comical movie shorts, or

13

picking up local girls in a nearby resort town. Stragglers came and went; surfers, photographers, musicians, and socialites would join the crew for a week or two then wander off at the next port or after the latest party. And of course Billy kept three or four women stowed away as housemaids on his yacht, replacing each of them as soon as his enthusiasm for her wavered.

He thought about their late-hour routine. After a full day of excitement they'd settle into their laidback ritual at the most secluded beach in the area, talk story, grind food, and get a good buzz on. Since Nathan had joined them three months into their trip, an evening custom had become the fireside rant; the guys would sit around playing music and experimenting with lyrics in front of the rolling sea. As the liquor, women, drugs, instruments, and surf stories mixed with the surreal sounds of the setting, blurred nights were spent wallowing in the shadowy pleasures of the underworld.

A part of him understood exactly what she meant, but the devil in him wanted the initial excitement to last forever. It was all becoming too much for Nathan to handle, but the sense of unlimited gratification was contagious. Sometimes he'd wake up the next morning still on the beach and other days he'd find himself back on the moored ship. One time the guys woke up floating in the powerless Zodiac surrounded by nothing but spacious ocean, and had to call on Kerby to find them because they'd passed out as the motor roared at full speed into the night.

Nathan's narrative made Nikki curious, reflective. She thought about the anguish she'd suffered for months after Kiri passed away, the torturous guilt at having wandered ahead of her

14

sister on that hike, and the promise she'd made one night after therapy to never leave her mum alone. A big part of her considered how liberating it would be to escape the internal stir. She sensed she could share anything with Nathan, but forced the unsettled emotions down below her carefree surface, choosing instead to live a few moments of pleasure.

They walked silently for a time, enjoying each other's company without the need for words. Turning her attention back to Nathan, Nikki grabbed his hand with a dreamy look in her eye. Her mind was working in overtime as it wandered somewhere beyond her field of vision. A master of the masculine personality, she sensed Nathan's inherent goodness, but was disappointed at how easily he had fallen into the reckless lifestyle.

Squeezing her hand tighter, Nathan said, "I wish I could share with you just how freeing it's been."

Trying to lighten her mood, she swung their interlocking hands high over their heads and back down again, stopped in her tracks, and finally said, "Sounds like the life I dream of. Wish I could get off this rock. Now don't you blokes go leaving before singing me a last song or two. I don't want to wake up tomorrow to an empty beach."

Nathan was honored. "You're making it hard for me to want to leave."

"Oh yah? And what do we do about that?"

"Well, I have an idea." He took a deep breath and let it out, "Why don't you come with us? I mean Billy's inviting girls on board all the time." He knew immediately that the last statement had come out all wrong.

She turned to him. "Don't get me wrong, I'd love to jump on board the tiki tour with the lot of ya'. But I'm not some piss-head that you and your pals can bonk for the thrill of it. I'll tell you that right now."

He took a sip of his beer. "Believe me, you can trust me. Ask anyone."

"Oh Luv, believe *me*, I'm not talking about you. I just don't know if I trust the rest of ya's."

He tried to stretch the truth, "They're good guys. They look out for me and treat me with respect."

"Oh, do they now?"

"And of course, they know how to have fun."

"That's what I'm afraid of. Especially that Billy character. I didn't get a good feeling about him."

Nathan had long ago been seduced by Billy's generous charm. "He's different than you think, Nikki, he's like a brother to me." He grew thoughtful. "Some nights the partying gets to be too much so he goes off by himself to read a book or write a few letters. Lately, he's been inviting me down to his cabin to come together on lyrics. And that's when we really talk about life; that's when I see what an incredible guy he is."

"Yah, good on ya both. I just don't want him to think I'm one of his women, I know how his kind works."

16

"Well, we do our own thing when we're not surfing. And anyway, you'll be with me most of the time won't you? So why don't you give me a chance and come with us?"

"We'll see my Luv. It's quite a tempting offer."

He looked around at the New Zealand coastline. "Could you leave all this beauty to be with a bunch of crazy guys for the next six or eight months?"

She replied sarcastically, "I've been waiting for my chance to get away for a time now." Taking a deep breath, she grimaced and began to think out loud, "My rellies would be a tad put out though. I've been in and out of trouble for a few years, but I'm a big girl now, graduated from University last spring and all. I'm the last one left of six children. My sibs went off all over the world to live their dreams and sow their oats." Her voice cracked as she paused and spoke under her breath, "Except Kiri of course." When she continued, she seemed to make her decision, "Believe me, I love mum and pop tons, but they'll get along without me for a while. I've taken my time because I know mum's gonna pack a wobbly when I finally decide to go on my way, and feel sorry for the old gal. She's taught me everything she knows about horses and riding, and all she wants from me is to find a good man and take over the ranch. But I believe it's time I explore the world a bit. We can always come back, am I right?"

As she finished the last sentence, Nathan felt a tingle from his head down through his toes. Her elegance had him under her spell, visions of a fairytale life flashing in his thoughts. She was the perfect answer to his dreams, as if she'd been set down amid the beautiful surroundings as a gift for the weary traveler. And to think, he had recently considered returning home to give his old life another shot.

She turned from him, began to mount her mare, and said, "Enough of this talk, it's just a pipe dream. Why don't we enjoy *this* night, for it may be all we have together. Jump on up, let's ride."

Nathan was disappointed by her indecision, but elated at her interest in him. Reaching out his hand to her, he said, "You're full of great ideas."

Off they rode across the pitch-black pasture, the chilly wind in their faces melting a nervous anticipation. After reaching a plateau, she allowed Yonkers to run free and their easy trot became a steady gallop. They bounded over a sloping hill and it felt as if they were flying, for she knew every inch of the land from blind memory. Focusing on her delicate shoulder blade, Nathan saw a line of tiny freckles resembling the Aquarian constellation. He leaned his head back, looking at the billions of stars overhead, and knew what it was like to be complete.

Her hair brushed his shoulder and he couldn't help but squeeze her waist tighter and inch closer to her bottom. She leaned back on him, stroked his head, and he felt her weight pressing against his shoulder. Then he heard her elegant voice begin humming softly in the breeze. She was too guarded to let out the words, but in her mind she sang about shadows of tall trees along the coast, her sister's faint voice calling in the darkness, and the sound of waves crashing in the distance. At once realizing her pleasing melody, he whispered, "Your tone is wonderful."

She slowed Yonkers' pace, looked toward Nathan with a wry smile and said, "Oh, did I forget to tell you that I sing a bit too?"

"Can I hear more?"

She teased, "Maybe later."

Nathan grabbed Nikki's arms and helped draw Yonkers to a stop at the edge of the cliff overlooking the beach fire. In his vulnerable state, he believed he was in love with Nikki Thomsen. But the reality of his longing was hard to put into words. It didn't matter that he'd just met her or that he may never see her again, all that mattered was they were together in this moment. As he pulled her off the saddle with playful intent, passion burned in his skin that he could no longer contain. Running his fingers up her loose blouse, he knew he was moving too fast, but couldn't control his desire to touch her. He leaned in to give her a kiss and she stopped him cold.

She pulled his hand away from her chest and snapped, "What do want me to do, drop my gear right here and let you give your ferret a good run?"

"What do you mean?"

"I mean slow yourself down, you randy sook."

He was throbbing with temptation, guilt, and disappointment. "I just thought I'd like to kiss you. I thought you might like that too?"

"I'll tell you what Nathan, slow down and get to know me first." She held both his hands to her chest and looked into his eyes. "And I just might go to the ends of the earth with you."

2.

The light of dawn radiated along the horizon as Nathan reached for Nikki's warm body, but got only a handful of sand. He looked around with glazed eyes and saw a thin line of smoke where the fire had been, realizing that he and Charge were the last two left on the beach. This reality shifted Nathan's mood, a twinge of morning melancholy replacing the joy from the previous night. His next dreadful thought was that she'd left for good, but he remembered how she'd spoken late that evening, which helped to lift his spirits.

He was beginning to realize how much of a toll the careless lifestyle was having on his body. He pulled himself up and stretched his back, shoulders, and legs, flexing his aching joints in preparation for the day's surf. Deciding she'd gone for a morning walk, he resolved to take the Zodiac up and down the beach to search for her before hitting the waves.

His head was pounding and he didn't feel like going alone, so he made it a point to wake up Charge in the quickest way possible. He grabbed a handful of sand and began pouring it into the ear of his hibernating friend. The oblivious warrior didn't move, as the pile overflowed out his ear and began settling on his cheek and beard. Then, after twitching his nose two or three times, the big man sat up with a start, looking as if he were about to kill. But when he saw Nathan standing over him, he simply laughed and asked, "Is it morning already?" He got up, shook the sand off his head and muttered, "Hell'uv'a a night, wasn't it?"

"Sure was. You mind going for a ride with me to search for a girl I met?"

"What girl?"

"A local girl. You must've been too drunk to remember. I'll tell you what though, she's something special."

"Oh yah? She better be. It's pretty damn early."

"Come on, you'll thank me for getting you up once we get in the water."

Nathan did everything but drag his buddy to the Zodiac, and in time, they shoved off the beach. While he searched the shoreline for Nikki from the craft, he wondered if she was thinking of him as she strolled alone next to the lapping waves. But after four or five passes up and down the coast, it was obvious that she wasn't there. Charge wasn't known for his patience when sporting a morning hangover, and was itching to get into the water. Demonstrating that cranky edge, he shouted, "I don't see no girl, bud. You sure you weren't dreaming?"

Nathan grinned at the man's grizzled appearance and said, "At this point, who knows. But I'll tell you what, I can't think of anything else right now."

"Listen, I'm goin' back to the *Rumrunner* so I can check out the surf. If you're still into her, you can come back before we take off."

With that, Charge grabbed the wheel of the inflatable and spun it with all he had, causing it to jerk to the right and abruptly change directions. He laughed at his sudden impulse of recklessness, thinking of the cool water that would lighten his headache. Minutes later, they were skipping past the rocky outcrop to where the ship was moored.

As they made their approach, Nathan feared he'd never see Nikki again. Regret swallowed him whole when he thought about what he'd do when Billy gave word to move out of their delightful spot. Would he have the courage to stop the ship, take the Jet Ski to shore, and knock on her door? And if she were there, would she go with him like they had discussed?

His worries subsided while climbing aboard when he saw her coming up from the lower cabin, looking like a goddess in a half open robe and white bikini bottoms. She seemed startled when she saw him, but grabbed his hands and explained that she needed a shower. He breathed a sigh of relief and didn't even notice the strange hush among the others who were kicking back in the dining area.

He gave her a cheerful glance through his uneasy frame of mind and said, "So you're coming out with us?"

"Yah, thought I'd give it a look. Took the morning off from the stables to see what the fun's all about."

He tried to sound settled as he said, "I just hope the waves hold up, it's looking kind of weak." He pointed out past the stern to their spot in front of the circular isle. It was the last day of the swell and big rollers were coming in, but they had little form or consistency.

Nikki raised her eyebrows and asked, "Do you wanna check out a place that gets crazy big on days like this?"

"Where at?"

She pointed to the open water. "Out there past Bell Block. We call it Mount Block. But I must tell you mate, it's a might intimidating with a swell like we've been having. In fact, I don't think most of the locals here have ever given it a go."

At that moment, Billy came from the lower cabin and patted Nathan on the shoulder. "What'll ya say? Your little friend told me about a secret spot past a shallow shelf a few miles out. Says her dad used to take her there to watch some huge breakers when she was a little girl."

Nathan felt something strange inside but tried to cover his murky suspicion by nodding towards Billy and Nikki.

The invitation had piqued the interest of the crew as well. After all, the theme of the trip was to explore uncharted treasures of the world. No one knew Billy's ultimate goal, but it was clear that he was on a quest for a new kind of freedom. Without question, he had a way of revving the gang to near frenzy, enticing images of that perfect wave in a flawless set.

So the guys scrambled to load their boards and gas up the Zodiac, while Gabriel, and Heather packed food, water, and beer into the cooler. Nikki tried to fit in by helping them, and remembered seeing the silhouettes of both girls competing for Billy's attention the previous night. She was mildly surprised that his young women were friends, working together without the slightest sense of rivalry. In fact, everyone on board seemed to share a bit of Billy's infectious energy.

Soon the seven of them were headed out past the point to the open ocean. The morning glow brought a special clarity to the

23

surroundings, revealing shades of blue found nowhere else except the oceans of heaven. Nathan took it all in, the lovely morning sounds, the sweet warm air, the crystalline water, the smooth touch of Nikki's skin pressing against his thigh. If only he could have placed that feeling of splendor under glass, or remembered how simple it was to achieve happiness, then he might have been better able to deal with the approaching emotions.

Billy was at the wheel for nearly ten minutes before he turned around and said to Nikki, "Unless you want to end up in South America, you better tell me where to go."

She rose from her seat beside Nathan. "Why don't you gim'me the wheel then. As soon as I find the channel, we'll be good."

"Hop on up here and lead the way."

Nathan felt another twinge of jealousy as she strolled up to the front and sat down on the edge of Billy's seat. She made a looping left and headed towards the horizon. Despite the four others crowded in the yellow boat, Nathan felt as if he were watching Billy and Nikki inside an intimate bubble. Watching the two of them make small talk together, he felt more alone then than at any time since stepping off the plane in Kauai. The wind blew her hair inches from his face, tempting him to reach out and touch it. But as he stared at her with miles of separation in his mind, she glanced back and grinned at him and he knew everything was alright. That smile of hers was contagious, instantly heightening his spirits-- he decided more than anything else, that pleasant way about her granted instant trust. He spent the rest of the boat ride watching his outstretched hand skip across the wake as he imagined the next time he would touch her.

A half hour later he saw the dark blue water turn to vibrant turquoise in a large oval-shaped bowl where an underwater peak had nearly climbed to the surface. The shallow spot allowed the surge to build in the deeper water and unleash its power along the outer ridge. There, they spotted the first set of fifteen-foot barrels breaking perfectly down the line in the outlying layers of deeper blue.

Nikki's predictions did not disappoint, as these were some of the biggest and cleanest waves they'd seen in months. She cut the engine just outside the break and the others raced to get in the water. Nathan asked if she was going to give it a go, but she told him after seeing their excitement, she'd rather watch them play. And anyway, with the size and thickness of the waves, it was best she stayed at the wheel to pick anyone up who might get into trouble.

During a lull between sets, Charge and Billy led the crew as they paddled out to the crash zone. As if Mother Nature was recharging herself, the air grew still and the water glassy. Waiting silently on the surface for nearly ten minutes, Nathan's heart began to race with anticipation of the waves' impending size and the idea of Nikki watching him. Her presence challenged him to compete against himself like never before. Yes, he had escaped to Hawaii to begin a life of oceanic adventure, but he'd begun the trip with little experience on anything other than Southern California slop. He had come a long way since those first few weeks of clumsy rides, but he had a long way to go to keep up with the others.

The initial set rolled upon them with intimidating force. True to his name, Charge was the first to paddle in, taking off late on the steepest part of the wave and barely making it to the bottom before being swallowed whole by angry jaws. A wide-eyed Heather took off on the next wave, finding her balance as she bee-lined it down the lip, then back up and out of the opening face. Nathan had paddled into the developing slope of each of the first two waves, but felt his will tremble and had to back off at the last instant each time. Garo was the next to try his luck, finding a smaller section of an in-between wave, and using a touch of finesse and fear to stay just ahead of the break, then bowing out before it crashed over him.

Nathan took a deep breath and told himself he was going to make the next wave. He found himself paddling side by side with Billy, in line for the final opportunity of the set. They stroked with all they had, struggling through the water's resistance to let them in, scrapping to join that exhilarating movement over the top. Just as he got in, Nathan realized he was too high on his board and was rolled under, tumbling through the air for infinite seconds before Billy raced right over the top of him as he vanished beneath the surface.

By the time he gasped through the spray and foam for his next breath, he heard his friends shouting at Billy for the incredible ride he'd apparently pulled off. It was true Billy Windsor was pure gold on his board, using waves as if they were his God-given right, gliding into tubes with grace and ease, yet able to find the power and speed at just the right moment to rip it up and bring it on home. Squinting at Nikki with salt-stained eyes just before another wave crashed on his head, Nathan saw her standing on the raft cheering for

26

Billy.  He shook his head in frustration and fear, knowing that he was in over his head in more ways than one, but refusing to accept it.

After the wipe out, Nathan lost his nerve, and for a time was unable to find the courage to paddle in.  Following two or three more near misses, he made his way back to the line-up with a new sense of urgency.  He felt the desperate need to slow things down, catch a breath, find his zone, and somehow impress Nikki.  Focusing with every fiber of his spirit, he visualized his path across the next rolling mountain.

The deafening giant bore in on him and he paddled with all he had.  He felt himself rising over the top and then dropping down the face with startling speed.  Trying to stay ahead of the point of impact, he leaned in hard and was thrust into the next open section, finding himself nearly inverted on the edge of the curling peak.  Grinning from ear to ear, he pulled off a floater and again tore down the face.  It was then that the tube hollowed out perfectly twenty feet overhead and sucked him in, swallowing him like that legendary white whale.

From the boat, it appeared as if Nathan were getting pummeled, for there was no way he could make the section.  But inside the huge barrel, he used its crackling power to rocket towards the light.  For a fraction of a second, he experienced a tranquility that seemed to come from the source, filling him with confidence and a sense of actualization.  A part of this sensation stemmed from his burning determination to make it out in one piece.  He looked down at the reef racing by only inches below the surface, glistening like a million sharp razors.  As the ceiling began to cave in on him, exploding fiercely overhead, he gave it all he had, leaning into the narrow slit while hanging on to the rail.

Nikki was the only one to see him shoot out the other side with his arms extended, shouting to the heavens. Nathan saw her raise her hand in triumph while filming the whole thing, and he believed his standing had changed for good. Without a doubt, it was the best wave of his life, yet the victory gave him a false feeling of confidence. In the past, his sharp caution and careful wave selection had allowed him to handle difficult surf, but now he believed he was only as good as his next ride. From then on, he would find fulfillment in the reckless abandon and close calls that might one day cost him his life.

The rest of the gang tried to catch their breath between sets and muster enough courage for one more ride, but the swell continued to come in with growing size and consistency. Gabriel and Heather both gave in to panic, paddling back to the boat before attempting a second ride. The three women had to drag a struggling Garo out of the water after a particularly violent blast cracked his board in two. Even Charge was put out of action after he was thrown into the shallows, opening a six-inch gash on his back. Of course he refused to go in at first, but after Billy noticed a nine-foot Mako shark circling the area, Charge climbed on in to get some medical attention.

By nine o'clock, no one was out there except Billy and Nathan. Throughout the mid-morning hours, the two of them caught waves rivaling the best Pipeline had to offer. But eventually, the tail end of the swell began producing closed out sets that were simply un-catchable.

They thought about going in, but Billy spotted a thin section of a rocky point that was still holding a speedy line. He pointed to the tube and said, "See that section about two hundred yards to the south? Think you can make that wave?"

Nathan, just happy to be hanging in there, was ready to go in. "I don't know, looks pretty brutal."

"Come on, give it a shot. You're surfin' like a star today."

The sun was beating down on their backs as they paddled through a lull to the new spot. Something had been rising in Nathan's mind since he got out there, an important point he had to clear up with Billy. But there had been little time for conversation because his focus was on staying alive. Between strokes, he saw this as his only opportunity alone with his friend and found himself taking a chance. Rather nervously, he asked, "So wha'da' you think of Nikki?"

Billy spoke of her as he spoke of all his women. "She's a pretty girl. Nice smile. Curvy body." Then he gave Nathan that sly glance, and said, "'Twill serve."

Nathan ignored the comment and pressed the issue. "Mind if she comes with us when we pull out of here?"

"Have I ever turned down a pretty face before?"

"No. But I'm asking for me this time. The rest of the girls are everyone's business. But I'd like to think of Nikki as off-limits to the rest of ya. I mean, I think I like this girl."

Billy nodded, "Of course, champ. The guys always said you were the lover boy type."

There was something more Nathan felt he needed to get out. Billy was starting to paddle into a steep wave as Nathan shouted, "I mean *you* too Billy!"

Billy looked back over his shoulder and smirked. "No worries, man. She's all yours." With that, he was on the wave, disappearing into the perfect curl with the ease of a graceful dancer.


Later that evening, the sleek vessel sped through the night, its foamy wake trailing in the darkness. Standing alone at the railing at three in the morning, Nathan felt a new sense of appreciation for what Billy had given him. And with Nikki now on board, he could enjoy every second of his nautical experience.

He looked down at the polished wood in his palms, admiring the detail in Billy's ingenuity. The 200-foot adventure craft was the finest the world had to offer, a marvel of modern design, craftsmanship, and luxury. Truly, it was an extension of Billy's far-reaching personality, an expression of his creative character. He'd spared no expense in building this pearl of the Pacific, hiring some of the finest designers and artists in the business to accentuate every curve.

Earlier, Nathan had taken Nikki on a tour to explore the ship, and she had nearly gotten lost in its elegance. He had allowed her to discover each of the vessel's striking features on her own, including the Vegas style game room, the mini theater, the art studio, the two-story library, the soundproof recording studio, and the drug warehouse complete with hidden entrance.

Of course, there was a 'First Nighters' club on the ship. Billy's goal was to indulge and challenge every new crewmate on board with his vision of fun, freedom, and enlightenment. After the tour, they enjoyed too many cocktails at the outdoor tiki bar at the stern of this ship. Nathan watched with pleasure as Nikki partied with the liberty of a gypsy and the exuberance of a comedian. Incessantly looking around at her new surroundings, she couldn't get over the architecture of her new hangout. For the first time in months, she was released from the heavy emotions of home. As the tequila flowed past the point of coherence, her words became slurred and she repeatedly commented on Billy's 'heavenly sanctuary.' Despite her drunken state, she was right, the area was awe inspiring-- complete with Roman pillars, marble flooring, contemporary statues, and topped with tropical accents sprouting from a jungle source.

Nathan was a bit worried about her, but knew there was little to do except hope she passed out soon. Her night had long become blurred when she began fixating on the source of the ship's waterfall. The tequila had heated up her insides, and she wanted to go swimming. Above the bar, two curved hot tubs were built into a magnificently engraved series of arches on the second deck. When she finally saw how their steady overflow fed the crescent shaped pool below with steaming cascades of water, she climbed the stairs and fell into the warm water while still fully clothed. The small crowd cheered as she then slid down the waterfall and began chasing Nathan through the middle of the greenery of the pool area.

Relieved that her night was coming to an end, he allowed her to catch him and they collapsed together in the sandy court of the volleyball net adjacent to the bar. She was laughing incoherently as he carried her down the stairs to his bedroom, and everyone knew that her initiation was complete. Yet, he was too much of a gentleman to take advantage of her.

It had been an entertaining night and Nathan was thrilled with their time together. Below deck, everyone had crashed out after overindulging in the festivities of the first night on the open sea. He tried to smile when he thought about how Billy would draw attention to her antics in the morning. Nathan understood how hard it was to keep up, because Billy was the only one who could find the energy to delve into *all* sides of pleasure. Another trace of uneasiness returned to his tired mind. He wondered how many women had been lured into the master suite only to wake up alone because he was out and about before dawn. Although envious of Billy's game, it felt good to have a woman to lose himself in, so he wouldn't have to clang with the revelers *every* night.

Feeling less than alone, he glanced up towards the tower and nodded at the captain, excited that Kerby was awake. Kerby Bonnato, aged beyond his thirty-one years, sometimes listened to Nathan's problems and confided traces of his past when alone at the wheel. Whenever Nathan was feeling off kilter, he'd visit the captain during his nightshift to discover a fresh ray of wisdom. Once the gruff man got rolling, he had an endless supply of mind-blowing stories, often using his remarkable series of tattoos as a guide. He'd spent the better part of fifteen years taking in as many life experiences as his body and mind would allow.

Nathan had recently gathered Kerby's fragmented connection to the *Rumrunner* through a series of sleepless nights. He learned how Billy had met him at a peer-side bar in San Francisco a few weeks before the trip, and let Kerby in on his dream of touring the world. Kerby shared his vast knowledge of the ocean with Billy, offering stories about his year on a fishing vessel in Alaska, his three months as a captain in the Greek isles, and various stints as a drug runner in the South Seas. The worn out traveler then explained how he'd been clean and sober for over six months after a speedball had nearly cost him his life. While recovering in a hospital in Amsterdam, he'd promised himself to focus on living life on different terms. This was just the type of character Billy wanted piloting his ship, so he offered Kerby the break of a lifetime with the agreement that he stay clean and sober while on board.

The somber man now motioned him up so Nathan climbed the narrow ladder to share his new situation. Kerby shook Nathan's hand and handed him the wheel. While gazing out to the deep, he spoke. "Can't sleep again?"

There was a long pause. "No."

"Why not?"

"The creative juices are flowing too strongly."

"Then why ain't you up in the crow's nest strummin' away on your guitar like you do?"

"Guess I'm too excited."

"Excited about that girl I've seen you with all night?"

"You got it. I can't write, can't play, can't read. She's all I think about."

"Then why ain't you with her right now?"

"Just taking it slow. We hung out on deck most of the night; you know how Billy is when we have a new passenger on board. When Nikki started to pass out, I gave her my room. Billy had four shots lined up for me when I got back to the bar, and the next thing I knew I woke up on the pool table about twenty minutes ago."

"The last nice guy on this ship, I think."

"Hey, I want to go back to my room and wake her, I want to make love to her until the sun comes up, but I respect her too much."

Kerby took a slug from a tiny silver flask, and put his finger to his lips to protect his little secret. He said, "Keep your head about you now, you got a lot going for you. Don't use all your youth up on some Kiwi out in the middle of the Pacific."

"But what I'm trying to tell you is I really like her."

"That's fine, my friend. But what I'm telling *you* is be careful or she'll hurt you. If you'd open your eyes, you'd realize you're in the prime of life. Enjoy it while it lasts, because once you let yourself go, you'll never get it back again. You take what you can get and keep going, keep getting all you can from every direction. And don't ever look back."

"I hear ya. But did you ever think about giving it up for a normal life? Did a girl ever do that to you?"

"No, but there were plenty I took along for the ride. What's the matter with you, don't you see what you got here?"

34

Kerby wasn't telling Nathan what he wanted to hear. He shot back, "Don't get me wrong, I've had more fun on this trip than I'll have the rest of my life. But..."

"But what?"

"But, I feel like I'm not doing anything with my life, like I want to make a difference somehow, some day. I mean I have everything I can dream of, but it's never enough. That is until I met Nikki. So I ask you, where are we headed? Why am I on this trip if I've found everything I'm looking for?"

"I was afraid you'd say that."

"Why?"

"'Cause you don't got it in ya."

"Got what in me?"

The weathered man got a gleam in his eye and replied, "A commitment to distinction and disgrace. The passion to be something more. See, the nut that invited you on this trip wants you to live life in a new order. He wants to push all of you to his level of genius and instability. He wants you to have it all."

"Why?"

"Don't you already know?"

"No."

With that, Kerby began to share Billy's astonishing family story. "See, that night at the bar Billy told me he liked me 'cause I remind him of his granddad when he was young. Says he used to stay up all night listening to Wild Willy sitting at the dining room bar, talking over the bitter voices of his parents in the next room, rambling on about how important it was to squeeze every drop of blood out of life."

For Nathan, the Midway moment suddenly became clear in his mind. "So he's doing all this because of his grandpa?"

"Yah, for his granddad's *legend*. In fact, the *Rumrunner* is named after him, a man who made his fortune smuggling liquor over the Canadian border during Prohibition. One of his favorite stories was the time the booze truck went through the ice on the Detroit River and his granddad had to float on an empty keg in the freezing water until the police arrived."

"Sounds crazy."

"Yah, the guy was the real deal. I guess he was able to meet with Capone and the boys a few times, and even took part in a few shootouts. But that was just the start of his wild life. The Big One hit and the son of a bitch became a war hero. When he returned from the Pacific, he played in a jazz band, dated movie stars, wrote books, drank like a fish, and gambled like a sieve. And when he had to run from the law, he did it with style, like in the old movies. He had plans to travel the world, but his health began to fail and he had to move in with his daughter. So anyway, Billy claims he always wanted the adventure he found in those wild stories, and when his parents died, he decided to go for it out of respect for the old man."

"I didn't even know his parents were dead. How'd they die?"

"Car crash. It seems they was in their Jag arguing over an account, when Mr. Windsor ran a red light and was broad-sided by an eighteen wheeler. Their client heard the whole thing over his speakerphone. Yah, Billy's parents took grandpa's money and created a hundred million dollar company, then killed each other trying to maintain it. So, Billy flipped his lid and decided to use his inheritance to model his life after his granddad's advice."

"OK, but why don't you think I have it in me to live at his level?"

"Because you still haven't told me why you're here talking to me tonight instead of down in your room with this girl you say you're crazy about."

Nathan was speechless. He thought about the disturbing feeling he woke with while alone in the game room. The gang had spent the early afternoon at Nikki's parents, trying to butter them up for her departure. Nathan was taken by the couple's hospitality and friendliness, as they genuinely seemed in love after years of marriage. He saw Nikki's beauty in her mother's Maori features and felt her charm in her father's English mannerism. They had lunch outside on the veranda overlooking the bluffs, feasting on lobster, white wine, and fresh oysters. But what caused him to lose sleep was what happened during dessert, when Nikki's loving energy began to wane. At one point Nathan seized up, sat back, and watched in disbelief. It was nothing more than a subtle glance at him, but he saw it just the same. The feeling of deception was impossible to explain.

No, it was ridiculous. The girl was into him, and he was afraid of her. He let go of the wheel, looked Captain Kerby in the eye, and spoke. "You know man, you're right. I need to just go for it."

"That's not quite what I meant."

"I don't care. She's on this ship to be with me."

"Alright, it's your life. But hey, watch yourself, you're a good kid."

He gave Kerby a strange look, nodded, and then climbed down the ladder to the main deck. There was a certain desperation in him, a frantic desire impelling him to see her immediately. He'd given up everything back home, a promising college career, the security of his fiancé, the good standing with his parents, to find what he was looking for, and now she was waiting for him on the other side of his door.

On the way to his cabin, he tried to plan what he'd say after waking her. He paused in the darkness, took a seat at the deserted tiki bar, poured himself a shot of tequila courage, then spent some time watching the engine's white trail in the moonlight. An image of the two of them holding each other in their arms and the anticipation of waking with her by his side drove him forward. He downed a second shot, took a deep breath, and was off.

Step by step, he forced himself down the stairs and up the hall. He lost his nerve at the last second and tiptoed past his cabin. Turning and standing face to face with the door, he saw a faint candlelight flickering under the frame. But when he heard her voice softly calling, he realized she wanted him to come in. He turned the handle and gently pressed his shoulder against the door, wondering how she knew he was there.

And there she was, in all of her glory. He took a double take as he saw her naked body on top of Billy's, legs straddling his midsection, hands clenching the bamboo headboard. Her back was arched at a lovely angle in the dim light, and if the devastation hadn't begun to drain his body of life, he might have been turned on. For over thirty seconds, he watched silently in the doorway while Billy filled her with his greatest talent.

At some point, his friend and mentor peaked out through her black hair and saw Nathan standing motionless in the doorway. He smiled at Nathan, grabbed her shoulders, and pressed her closer to his chest. She looked over her shoulder and their eyes met for an instant; then she quickly looked down to the sheets, searching for an answer to her drunken shame. Nathan just turned and walked away, empty of any reaction, void of all emotion. As he jogged back up the stairs, he heard Billy laugh and say, "Hey Nathan, there are no rules to love and war, am I right?"

Billy and Nikki didn't catch up with him until he'd nearly reached the bow of the ship. They followed at a safe distance until they saw him punch and kick at rigging and railings. When he sliced his hand open on a wire cable, Billy stepped in. Piling on an extra helping of his charm, he patted Nathan on the shoulder and said, "Come on man, it's all fun and games until someone gets hurt."

Nikki, wrapped in nothing but a silk sheet, tried to sooth him with garbled words. He felt a bit of satisfaction in the fact that she looked pretty shaken up by the whole thing. She approached with her head hung low and said, "I'm so sorry Nathan. Don't take this personally. You just don't understand." He began to walk away, but she stopped him, her sheet slipping briefly enough for him to get a hint of tan line on her breast. "Come on, give me a chance to explain."

He wanted to hear what she had to say, but refused to give in. Instead, he turned and started walking towards the bridge. Billy, who was losing his buzz and getting impatient, grabbed him by the back of the shirt, spun him around, and said, "Stop man, it's not her fault. I wouldn't have went for her if I knew you'd get so shook up over it."

Nathan could do nothing more than laugh in his face, so Billy gave him a little shove out of disrespect. Letting loose with aggravated reflexes, Nathan popped him in the nose. Having quickly turned the tide, he made a motion to unleash all his fury on his ex-friend, but out of the corner of his eye he saw Nikki step up to defend. He had no other choice than to run with all his might and hide in the one place that he would never be found.

Just before leaping out over the front railing, he looked back and shouted, "You two are fucking perfect for each other." Then he made the twenty-foot dive, barely clearing the hull as he slipped through the wake where dolphins often played. It wasn't that he was necessarily trying to kill himself, it was just in that piercing moment he didn't care what was going to happen next.

All was peaceful as he stared up at the midnight-blue water while the ship's massive underbelly passed directly over him. He sank and was instantly out of breath, but didn't panic because his thoughts turned to the day he met Billy and the crew. Billy had seemed to come from nowhere to rescue him that first morning in Kauai, and up until now Nathan had revered him as some kind of a hero. Vivid memories of those first few months on board (and that first night with Nikki) made him feel a sense of tranquility, despite the fact that he was gulping water like an eel. He wanted nothing more than to fade into nothingness while reliving the memories of the good times.

In the grave moments before losing consciousness, his mind didn't care that his body was giving out, but an instinctive will to survive began to take over his limbs. Something from deep down told him to kick his legs with all his might, and his numb mind followed the distorted moonlight to regain the surface. With bubbles pouring out of his mouth and nose, he shot up headfirst and watched the double props pass inches from his face. In this critical moment of survival, Nathan made an even more important choice, deciding to *live* a different existence.

3.

Charge was yanked out of his stupor by Nikki's wild screams. Stumbling to the main deck, he tossed Nathan a lifeline. While he pulled in the sad sack of lead, the drowsy man shouted, "Nice stunt, dick face. I'll tell you what though, this is gonna be the last time I save your ass."

As he grabbed the line, Nathan remembered the other time he'd been pulled in by Charge, after facing serious doubts as to whether he'd survive his first day in Hawaii. The drama leading up to his chance meeting with the *Rumrunner* was now nothing more than a comical legend, told each time with an added twist of outrageous misfortune by Billy and the guys. But for Nathan, the story was a haunting memory that still lingered under the surface of his insecurities.

From the moment he stepped off the plane and onto the breezy runway, catching the first hint of that sweet Hawaiian air, he knew his goals would never be the same. Armed with nothing more than his favorite surfboard, a weathered Gibson, and an oversized backpack, he set out toward the northern coast of Kauai chasing his dream of music, all the while trusting a sense of imminent adventure. As he walked over curving roads cut through the hills, he felt a release from his reserved upbringing. More than once, he wondered how his parents were handling his decision to walk away from everything.

He paused to watch the sun disappear in a kaleidoscope of pink, violet, and orange curls. The island flora invigorated his lungs, its fragrance pumping self-assurance through his bloodstream. For the first time in years, he felt excited by his surroundings, empowered by the naiveté of the unknown. In time, he made his way into an isolated stretch of forest. His creative energy was stirred by the remoteness, the calming beauty building to inspiration. Strands of melody and snippets of vocals gathered, fluttered, and then galloped through his thoughts. Overcome with expression, he sat down on an ancient-looking rock wall and began to play his guitar. Unrefined insight and raw lyrics eased out of his mouth and combined with a series of simple chords.

Nathan was too hypnotized by his rush of expression to react to a beat-up Toyota pick-up that screeched to a halt on the narrow shoulder beside him. Its high-beam headlights forced him to look up from his focal point, and three sets of white teeth shined at him through heavy black air; three shadowy Hawaiians glared at him out a tinted window. In his other life, Nathan would have froze, sensing the approaching danger, but his new mind-set welcomed the interaction. His thought was that the young men would open him to stories of their culture.

The smallest of the locals looked irritably into Nathan's eyes and spoke. "Hey dummy, what you doin' way out here by yourself at night?" Then he scoffed at his buddies and muttered, "Dumb Haole."

Nathan answered in a steady voice. "I'm just trying to make my way to the Na Pali Coast to catch some surf."

"Then you best get you'self some protection or someone's gonna jump your ass."

"Hey man, I'm not looking for trouble."

The two others snickered wise comments in their sharp pigeon tongue, making a series of threats that they may or may not have carried out depending on their target's reaction. But a forth local, a huge Samoan with springy hair, stood up in the bed of the cruiser. The weight of the vehicle shifted to the right as he leaned over the wheel well and said, "Cool it down up there, man, I like this bra-dah's style." He extended his hand and continued, "Hop on up. We give you ride to de end of de road, we' goin' up that way anyhows."

Something told Nathan to get in, maybe a certain stillness in the air assuring him he could trust the big man. As he climbed over the tailgate, stepping on a large machete lying on the floor, he realized how badly he wanted everything to be all right in his world, convincing himself of the inherent goodness of man. Although his stepfather's ways would die hard, a new personality was being conceived in him, an easy going 'no worries' way of thinking where everyone had purpose and everything had reason. All the new age books he'd read when he was supposed to be studying must have made a difference because he was no longer afraid of the inevitable disappointment that people brought him.

He sat down next to the bulking man, facing the darkness stretched out behind them. The truck sped off and made a quick turn about a quarter mile up the road, bouncing onto a dirt trail cut through green hills and rocky pastures. Wind filled Nathan's hair and blew it back into his eyes, while leafy branches brushed the body and roof of the speeding pick-up. He leaned his head against the back window and closed his eyes, exhausted from the flight, reflecting on the circumstances that brought him so far away from his family's plan.

As Nathan looked up at billions of brilliant stars filling him with confidence, he heard the wind say, "Where you at anyhow, brah?"

Taken aback, he looked into the fat man's eyes and muttered, "Huh?"

"I said, 'Where you at?' You not here wit me, dat's for sure."

"I was just thinking."

"Well, come back to me, brah-duh. Why don't you tell me who you are and what you're doin' here tonight?"

Mustering enough social graces to pull himself back into the moment, he said, "I'm Nathan Jansen, and I've come out here...just to get away."

"Nice ta' meet you, Na'tan."

"You too."

"I'm Kalaka. But my friends call me Koko. You know what dat means?"

"No, what?"

"It means 'blood' brah, my friends call me Hawaiian Blood."

"Good to know you, Koko."

The fat man's temper rose, "No, you mean you're *lucky* to know me. Hawaiians don't like pale haole's walking around at night messin' wit their land. You lucky I lookin' out for you tonight or da boys would'a had their way wit you."

"Thanks man. I'm glad you picked me up, but I ain't messing up no one's land. I just came out here for a backpacking trip along the Coast."

Koko's tone changed from intimidating to concerned. "You shouldn't go bu, not at night. You don't want to be out there at night. You gonna get jumped."

"Should I still be worried about your friends in the front?"

Koko's face was cold and serious. "Nah brah, something much worse come out ta' get you."

"I don't understand."

"Listen. Ya best watch yourself ova' there on da trail, huh? It taboo. Kaupo! Night marches come fo' your ass."

"What?"

Koko's voice grew more intense and his accent became more dramatic, "Dey da spookies. Old Haw-vi-ans dat don't sleep at night no mo'. *Ala hou anna*! *I'm talking resurrection.* I tell yu again, don't go hiking dat trail at night-time."

"What are they?"

He pointed into the darkness. "They's da young men dat didn't survive manhood training back in da kine. Jump off da cliff with a big rock and neva' come back again 'til they dead. Nightmarchers climb dose cliffs at night brah-dah, and bring yu ass down wit dem."

"Well shit, maybe I'll just hang out with you guys till morning. What're you up to anyway?"

Koko began to laugh as if the whole thing might be a joke. Then his eyes lit up and he answered, "We goin' up to La Pakka's cottage to have some drinks and smoke some stuff. You come along?"

Nathan shook his head and began to feel a sense of security in his new friendship. The pick-up bounced its way onto a windy, vertical path. The trail was overgrown with tropical darkness, and he could see the guys up front searching for a hidden driveway. Koko took out a bottle in a brown paper bag and offered Nathan a drink. Then he reached over, put his arm around Nathan, and patted him gruffly on the shoulder. "I see you play the guitar, brah." He began to hum a soft tune in Hawaiian while tapping his knee to an ancient

46

rhythm. His voice was low and soothing, as he exaggerated each syllable of the words he sang, "Akaka hoo-le-mana, wale ma-ke i-lina…"

Despite his enormous size and rough exterior, a softer side was coming out, as if he were an embarrassed child trying to share a secret with Nathan. At first this shift in personality was reassuring, an authentic cultural experience, but he soon grew uncomfortable. They approached a clearing on top of a hill and Nathan could see a dim light outlining a rustic window. Koko sighed with nervousness and asked, "When we get there, you wanna come wit me out back to the shed?"

A hollow terror shot through Nathan's bloodstream, churning his stomach, shriveling his testicles. At once he understood the dangerous situation he'd gotten himself into. He felt a panicked need to get out of the truck and fumbled to pick up his pack, but instead grabbed Koko's ankle. Every nerve ending in his body froze as he looked up to the predator with a shocked expression.

The glutinous man saw the terror in his eyes and said, "Hey bu, I may be a big horny Hawaiian, but I ain't crazy. Why don't you lie back there and I help you relax."

Nathan tried to say, "No thanks," but the words wouldn't come from his mouth. His mind whirled. He had one shot at life or death. The beast squeezed him tighter, reached for an exposed knee and began to run his lumpy hand up Nathan's thigh. He went on, "See, there's another reason dey call me Koko. Lie back, I show you."

This last statement thawed Nathan's rubbery sinews, unwound years of wound-up tension, sent a rush of adrenaline through constricted limbs. He burst up like hell's explosion, slicing through Koko's chin with an elbow. In one movement he was up and out of the moving truck, but realized while tumbling to the ground that he'd forgotten his gear. The truck slammed on its brakes and skidded to a stop. Koko was stunned, but madder than a bull. Nathan made it back to the truck just as the wild man climbed on top of the wheel well. Before Koko could leap on him, Nathan grabbed and yanked his fat ankles with all his might, sending him crashing backwards on the rusty floor. The three vagrants up front might have hit their head's on the ceiling from the impact of the crash.

As Nathan ran down the road with armfuls of his possessions, he saw a long metal blur wiz by, inches from his ear, whirling end over end. The machete made a thud as its blade stuck in a eucalyptus tree just as Nathan escaped into thick flora. He ran awkwardly down hill for about thirty seconds then dove into the densest underbrush he could find, using his arms for additional cover. He heard the truck spin around and crash into his entrance point. Headlights glared and high beams flashed in his direction. A single ray of light gleamed on his forehead, so he sunk down on his haunches and closed his eyes. He heard the four guys shouting and howling at the moon, but their voices were trailing off down the far side of the hill.

Their next threat would approach from below the road, so Nathan doubled back up hill towards the cottage, finally pausing on the edge of the clear-cut property. After several minutes of heavy breathing, he found the courage to move past the open yard and disappeared into the other side of the dark rainforest.

He reached the Kalalau trail just after midnight. Facing him was the most spectacular coastal landscape on American soil, eleven miles of rain-forested cliffs, hidden sea caves, ocean side waterfalls, and secluded beaches. But beauty would have to wait, because the moist air made him feel as if he were walking through layers of black silk. He looked over his shoulder, thought he saw shadows following him, then got out his flashlight and chased its high beam into the unknown, inching his way on the narrow trail one step at a time. Progress was slow and his feet quickly became raw from the sharp lava-rock ripping through gnarled flip-flops. But, the pain was dulled by his terror. His body told him to rest for the night, but he forced himself to make his way as far as his legs would carry him, for the haunting image of Koko had seized his nerves.

After climbing for nearly twenty minutes, he reached the first crest, pausing as the full moon peaked over a distant summit, brightening the sky and exposing five hulking silhouettes along the coast. The massive cliffs stood at attention in the dim light, immense rock faces staring down over the water in defiance, their mysticism calling to him. He pressed on, and for a time was able to focus his thoughts on nothing more than the challenge of his next step. About a mile in, his pace stabilized enough to remind him of what had happened earlier. Shame overcame him, followed by a sense of self-loathing, and finally a deep twinge of anger. Profanity burst out his crooked lips as he promised himself never to be manipulated like that again.

The mixed emotions forced him to near exhaustion while the dread in Koko's warnings came back to get him. The dirty pig had sounded so believable when he spoke of ghosts on the trail. Nathan suddenly understood the aching despair of being alone. Seclusion can be a terrible thing, especially when you're used to the ceaseless interactions of the everyday. And on this night, Nathan Jansen began to feel the isolation caused by the walking dead. He rationalized that Koko had created this fear in his mind, but it wasn't enough to calm his razor sharp perception of the surroundings. He began to hear unfamiliar noises deep within the forest, voices calling down from between the overhangs, and gurgling grunts below the surface of the moonlit sea.

Unable to stand the silent anticipation a second longer, he heard himself call out, "Hello?!"

The verbal outburst echoed through the night air, and Nathan's soul was stilled. He grabbed his guitar and gave in to the fear, closing his eyes and playing without a care in the world. Standing erect in the darkness at the cliff's edge, facing the sea three hundred feet below, he allowed more of his repressed creativity to escape. In that moment, he played for the ocean, he played for the island, he played for himself.

He strummed powerful chords with freedom and grace and the atmosphere allowed for a natural progression in his music. Rhythms he'd never dreamed of escaped his fingertips. He played with such joy that it felt like the first time, as if this moment was a rite of passage to another world.

As long as he played, there was no fear, sadness, or confusion because life made sense. But gradually, the inspiration faded, and he grew more and more exhausted. He lay down on the ground facing the black sheet, one arm hanging off the edge of the bluff.

A short time later he was startled awake when he heard sharp voices calling for him from the other side of the tree line. The fear crept back into his brain, as his weary thoughts told him nightmarchers were rising up from the expanse to pull down into their depths. But then he distinctly heard Koko's deep voice shout into the silence, "You can't run forever, bu. The trail ends up there and we come and get you."

Nathan grabbed his gear, took one step towards the vista and tripped over an exposed root. He fell face first into a shallow stream, landing on his surfboard. Before he was able to react, he was sliding over the embankment. He held onto his board for life as it bounded down the steep black rock, spilling out fiberglass resin with each shattering impact. The last hundred feet was a sheer drop, so Nathan let go of his board and flipped head over heels in the air, landing feet-first in the warm water. When he surfaced, he watched his guitar, a gift from his parents for his thirteenth birthday, hit a crevice and splinter on a jagged rock. His backpack was swinging from a tree branch like a leopard's fresh kill, two-thirds of the way up the face.

He tried to gather his composure, but saw nothing but inaccessible coast for miles in both directions. His adversaries had caught a glimpse of his graceful exit, and appeared at his cliff-side camp. They stood on the edge hooting and hollering at him, applauding with laughter. Koko called down, "Havin' a nice trip, brah-dah? Why don't you climb yo' ass back up here, I make it worth your while."

Nathan could do nothing more than flip him off. The bullish man picked up Nathan's abandoned journal and started to tear out pages full of songs and poems, crumbling them up and tossing them one by one into the sea. Then he paused and said, "What's this here?" Snickering, he called for silence and read one of the entries out loud. "Let's see. 'Love thoughts. They scratch and they bite, infect me with all her might, so I take her back again, again, and again.' Now that's touching, brah. You *sure* you're not a homo?"

The others laughed and began pelting Nathan with rocks. When a sharp sliver of lava grazed his shoulder and stuck in his board, he had no other choice than to paddle out to the open blue. He decided his best chance was to try to make it all the way to the campsite at Kalalau Beach eight miles to the west.

He'd been struggling in the ocean currents for more than two hours when Billy's splendid ship appeared on the skyline. By midmorning, Charge had fished him out with a line and a giant fishhook, leaving his surfboard bobbing like a bloated tuna. As the shaken and exhausted man lay panting on the deck, Billy shot a few wisecracks and asked, "Is there any reason why I shouldn't throw you back to the fish?"

Nathan looked up through teary eyes and said, "Well, I can play the guitar."

And that's how their friendship was born. As he sat at the bar, downing shot after shot, telling the crew his chilling story, they laughed themselves off their barstools. Billy raised his glass in a toast, giving a salute before telling him he could stay on his ship as long as he liked. Within hours, Nathan felt so comfortable singing and playing with the guys, it seemed he'd been a part of the trip from the beginning.

But now, as Charge lifted him over the railing with that same long pole, it was gut wrenching to even think of getting back on board to face Billy and Nikki. His best friend and his new lover were nothing more than his enemies. Looking Nikki in the eye as she stared back with her arm around that traitor, he promised himself things would never be the same.

4.

If invited to spend a few hours hanging out on the *Rumrunner*, a modern psychologist might ask, "What is courage in this world of selfish extremes? Is it helping others through danger, pain, and uncertainty or challenging yourself to do what you never thought you'd dare?" For those following Billy's lead, there was never a lack of bold daring, but too often a shortage of heroic deeds.

A shivering Nathan shook Charge's hand for saving his ass again, then stormed away and climbed to the highest point of the ship to hide his shame. His boy-like sensitivity had been crushed. Crouching on a thin cable above the crow's nest with tears welling in his eyes, he felt isolated enough to release his sorrow.

The good life was all but over; the two people closest to him had stabbed him in the back. And who was to blame? *Billy*. Respect for that dirty bastard drained from his mind like the blood from a blooming ghost. He thought back to those times between sets in the studio, when Billy would pull him aside and toss around some lines he'd been working on describing modern civilizations and world harmony. The power in those raw lyrics made it seem like anything was possible while they played together. But Billy was nothing but a hypocrite because although he talked a good game, rambling on about a higher state of mankind while strung out on coke, he was unable to live up to his own pathetic expectations. Now, after watching Billy take her away, Nathan knew their dream of a musical revolution was nothing but nonsense.

And then there was Nikki. He might get over Billy's lack of boundaries, but there was no escaping her betrayal. She was the woman he may have been willing to give his life to, and the devastation ran deeper than the days before he left his old life. Yet, something remained inside, for he couldn't get her soothing voice out of his mind. As asinine as it sounded, he couldn't bring himself to give up hope that one day he'd be with her. She was the sweet mana drawing him away from everything that made sense, and he'd chase her energy to the ends of the earth.

But why didn't she want him? What was wrong with him? He blamed himself, channeling the rejection from his music and social life into her betrayal. And although it was too soon to realize, the harmony and tranquility of the good life was becoming galvanized into an empty longing to impress her at any cost.

Nathan remained isolated in the crow's nest for the better part of three days. From his post, he'd watch subtle changes in the ocean's patterns, losing himself in the blue currents while dwelling on his dark thoughts. He spent the endless hours of sunlight strumming his guitar and pouring over frenzied lyrics. The nothingness surrounding him wouldn't let him sleep, and he began to feel as if he was losing touch with reality. He'd sneak down at times during the night, load up on food, booze, and weed, then swipe whatever personal items he could find of Billy's as a pathetic attempt at revenge.

Feeling especially desperate on the third night, he found himself stumbling down the hallway to Billy's suite. He peaked into the lavish room, and from the reflection in the closet mirror caught a glimpse of Nikki's toes curled around Billy's muscular calf. Overwhelmed with jealousy, Nathan looked down at his trembling hand and realized he was brandishing a ten-inch fishing knife.

He rushed back to his hideaway, climbed the rope ladder, and threw the knife into the dark sea. He began to hyperventilate, and between gasps of air realized that his mindset would have to change. Soon, he drifted off into a disconcerted slumber, and for the first time since leaving home, longed for the comfort of his own bed.

Nathan awoke before dawn with the jagged silhouette of Lord Howe Island facing him in the distance. As they approached the wondrous gem off the eastern coast of Australia, he was astonished at the razor green cliffs jutting out of the ocean's surface. The breathtaking views gave his bewildered emotions a long needed sense of relief, conveying the message that his only chance at salvation was to become a better man.

The ship was anchored just outside the crescent shaped lagoon outlining the length of the island, and he watched his friends stirring with the rush of new adventure. He wished he could again be a part of it. Just before Charge boarded the Zodiac, he shouted up to Nathan. "Hey *Willful*, are you ready to get your heart out of your ass and have some fun?"

The others began to wave him on and soon were chanting his name. Nathan wanted to come down and act as if nothing had happened, pretend things were the way they used to be. He was excited to get a chance to speak with Nikki. But when he saw Billy grab her from behind, grope her breasts, and toss her off the back deck into the clear water, that nauseating feeling dropped back into the pit of his stomach. He knew he wasn't ready to be the bigger person.

With his binoculars, he watched them carousing, snorkeling, exploring the coastline, and was sickened by his isolation. He narrowed his sights on Billy and Nikki hanging on each other as if they were on an exotic getaway. Unable to take another minute of their affection, he climbed down and slipped into the recording studio. There, he found an outlet for his bottled-up infatuation. Most songs he'd recorded were light-hearted and laidback, fun little ditties highlighting their lifestyle. But now he played with a piercing desperation that was maddening to the ears. Most of it was a whole lot of garbage, but at times his dark portrayals of loss echoed the themes from Seattle's emerging grunge movement. The problem was, he just couldn't put anything together because his stormy emotions wouldn't be contained.

The crew wallowed in their glory on the beaches of Lord Howe for a couple of days, allowing Nathan the latitude to play with his new style. But Billy grew bored of the tiny island because few people lived there and he couldn't find any unique gifts for his lover. So when Nathan saw the Zodiac heading back towards the ship, he climbed back up to his isolation post. From there, he heard Billy give a bleak surf forecast for Blinky's, the only decent surf spot on the island. Twenty minutes later, the ship was headed northeast towards the next group of wonders.

Watching Nathan scamper up the ladder, Billy seemed to find the whole situation hilarious. So he made a childish game out of the strained interactions with his friend. When he was hopped up, he'd climb up to the crow's nest and sit within inches of Nathan's face, or wait for him to come down and follow him around the main deck, or hide below deck and jump out to startle him in front of the others. In his own way, he was actually trying to apologize by using outlandish tactics. But when Nathan refused to respond, Billy grew worried he might bring down the group's vibe, and began to consider dropping him off at the next major port.

Nathan continued to go into the studio each night. Although somewhat soundproof, the thin walls couldn't contain the power in his surge. He'd ceaselessly pound the drums for an hour straight, then lay into the electric guitar with reckless abandon. Late at night on the open ocean, Garo heard the violent chords bleeding through to the dining room and recognized their potential. He knocked on the door, and after much haggling, talked Nathan into allowing him to join the jam session. They smoked some heavy stuff and for the next twenty-four hours barricaded themselves in the musical bunker, tinkering with dozens of sounds. Garo used his talent to infuse Nathan's unrefined creativity with intention and order. And by the time they reached Norfolk Island, the exhausted two-some had produced 'Challenge Me', a gritty tune about taking one too many risks and crossing the line of death.

That evening, Nathan bumped into Nikki on the main deck. A fire flickered in his eyes and a smile appeared on his face as he walked past her, for pain had become his ally. Sure, the no-limits jam session had expanded his musical know-how, but it did something more as well. Suddenly, he understood the absolute release he'd find when putting his new philosophy into action.


They remained anchored near the northern bluffs of Norfolk Island for almost a week, the final destination for the notorious *Bounty* descendents. Billy was the only one excited about this tiny speck in the Pacific, as he claimed a 'can't miss' swell was headed towards Anson Bay. But truly he was there to fill the gaps of his nostalgic attraction to the legendary castaways of Pitcairn Island.

The crew began grumbling that the waves were flatter than a windowpane, while the color of sea was turning an ugly shade of brown. And Billy was acting strange as he insisted on making day trips to the island alone to gain knowledge for his personal rebellion. Charge finally approached him on the morning of the third day and asked, "Billy, what the hell are we sticking around here for? You go talking to old men and women every day and there's nothing for us to do. And haven't you noticed that the water is a deep shade of diarrhea?"

"That may be true, but have *you* noticed how it glows at night?"

"Yah, so?"

With his fascination of marine biology, Billy surmised that a toxic algal bloom had hit the area, explaining that millions of microscopic phytoplankton were thriving in the stagnant shallows. He said, "The toxins might make us pretty sick if we swim in them, but it's a sign of the sea's revival. And if I were a superstitious man, I'd think that good times are ahead. Something big I'd guess."

It was clear that Billy wouldn't leave, banking on the approaching swell and content to learn firsthand stories of the mutinous way of a life that he was so drawn. But Charge persisted. "Billy, I'm not interested in any of your horseshit. We can't surf, can't even go in the water. And hell, you're getting funny about letting us off this boat to talk to the locals."

It was then that Billy caught Nathan peaking at him from the post, listening to their whole exchange. He looked up and asked, "Spying on us are you?" With a mind clouded by paranoia, exhaustion, and his current obsession, he pulled from his knowledge of the disturbing legend. "Who do you think you are, Fletcher Christian? What's this all about buddy, you planning to lead a band to mutiny? Tie me up, throw me overboard, and divvy up the spoils yourself?"

Nathan looked away without comment. He was comfortable taking on Billy with silence. Yet, he also realized that if he didn't make amends, he'd be left behind for good. No one seemed to care about his extended absence from the scene, because the crew winced at anyone who felt sorry for himself. Nathan dreamed of a mutiny, but knew his revenge would have to come from a more subtle approach.

He smiled at Nikki and the others who had gathered around the scene. "Alright, I'll tell you what, if the swell doesn't come tonight, we'll leave in the morning. I don't want the lot of ya' pulling a Captain Bligh on me."

Billy decided to camp on the beach that night and Nathan remained isolated aboard the ship. The guys got good and wasted that evening as had become their ritual the night before departure. They talked long into the night, and eventually lay down together around the smoldering campfire. But Billy woke at four in the morning to the sound of the point break coming alive.

After glancing out over the spot, he invaded Charge's sleeping bag, shook him silly and said, "Wake up dummy!"

"Huh…what the?"

"Get your ass out'a bed I said. The swell's here."

Charge let one rip, rolled over, and muttered, "It'll still be here in the morning."

"Yah, but you gotta see this."

"This better be good."

Soon, they were gathered along the beach looking out over the dark horizon. Nathan was nowhere to be found. The swell had rolled in with fierce intensity, and the show it was putting on was something out of a science fiction film. An invasion of Red Tide is an ugly spectacle, crystal clear water drowned in bloody brown, resembling the aftermath of a horrible naval battle. But anyone who has seen its wonder at night understands nature's ironic rewards. The curling waves were actually *glowing* with phosphorescence, a stark contrast to the surrounding blackness. Each line of breakers was a brilliant aquamarine, as if a florescent light had been turned on inside, shimmering and sparkling with such brilliance that they seemed to break in midair. A few of the girls gasped and one of the guys gulped. And when Nikki pointed to the next wave, a shadowy figure was seen moving through the radiant tube.

For Nathan, getting lost in a glowing tunnel was like entering a dream world. As he peered through the black channel, he saw the fins of his board cutting the waves with precision, leaving a glistening trail. He was able to intuitively see the next turn, sense the next dip, as if he were riding a roller coaster with his eyes closed. The gang cheered him on with pleasure and wonder, the second time in less than a month he'd found his identity in the surf. Only now, Billy was nothing more than a spectator, compelling Nathan to believe he'd finally outdone his rival.

By the time the others had paddled out, dawn's light was breaking, and the aura of the gleaming waves had faded. When they reached him, his friends revered him like a champion. Even Nikki paddled out on a pink long board to congratulate him. Later, while reflecting on the ride, Garo recalled a cave full of florescent worms they had explored in New Zealand. There were smiles all around when he looked at Nathan and coined the nickname, "Glowworm."

So Nathan was again a part of their vicious cycle, savoring his new status like an emerging superstar while bringing the crew into an age of 'No Limits.' Billy was impressed by the performance, excited that Nathan was challenging himself to become his Fletcher Christian. And from that moment on, Nathan wanted nothing else out of life but to go beyond the boundaries of extreme, to show Nikki that he was indeed, a man.

5.

Billy's formal apology came later that night when Nathan stepped into his room and found Gabriel and Heather tied together to his bed with laced lingerie. A small mirror sat on the foot of the bed displaying two glow-in-the dark condoms and a heart made of cocaine. Nathan couldn't hold back his laughter when he saw that the powdery design was framing a small yellow pill with a smiling worm engraved on it. Each of the girls had already taken a hit of Ecstasy, so he had no other choice than to suspend his morals and give into temptation, popping the pill and then doing a few lines.

Minutes later, every nerve was dancing in his skin, his senses overloaded with lips, breasts, nipples, and thighs. And for the next four hours, he released mountains of pleasure and fury while entangled in their sensual bodies. The girls were brilliant at teasing and torturing him into a state of bliss, sometimes taking turns while one watched and other times joining in together. And as Nathan faded with exhaustion into the early morning hours, he thought his liberation from Nikki was complete.

By the time he awoke in the late afternoon, he'd buried his feelings for her so deep that he felt like a different person. And the boost of confidence almost made it seem as if everything were back to normal on the ship. But one thing had grown clear in his mind, there wasn't a better time to live or die.

Billy had again changed plans and decided to check out the sights and sounds of the islands surrounding New Caledonia. So the others had no other choice but to enjoy the ride while traveling from isle to isle, searching for undiscovered surf spots, interesting nightlife, and unusual gifts for Nikki.

Nathan still spent a lot of time in the crow's nest, enjoying views of the uninhabited atolls dotting the ocean like green clouds of the deep. There, his creativity was continuously stirred by hills shaped like animal tracks, whale humps, and grassy sombreros. One morning, he spotted an exquisite cove surrounded by rows of tall, thin pines rising from the shoreline on the most secluded of the Loyalty Islands.

Billy grabbed Nathan and the two of them took the Zodiac to check out the waves. But as they passed by the white sand beach, the only sets they saw were the heaving black breasts of three young, grass-skirted women running out to the shallows to greet them. They were Kanaks, dark-skinned locals with ancient links to the Aborigines. Their clan had decided to escape French influence and get back to their cultural roots. Billy remembered hearing their name linked to cannibalism and saw the prospect of visiting the village as an exciting new escapade.

Upon making landfall, they were greeted by a dozen children looking up to them with mouths agape. Billy exchanged some chocolate for a Kanak necklace, then gained instant hero status when he handed out a few of his beat-up surfboards and motioned that he'd teach them how to ride the waves. The locals thanked him, using a combination of gestures, broken English, and Kanaky dialect. Their reaction prompted him to settle there for a night.

Billy burned the day away bartering with the friendly natives, trading liquor and hash for exotic jewelry, bizarre artifacts, and exquisitely carved idols. Once rolling, he masked his personality like a chameleon, becoming an instant favorite with the Kanaks while soaking in their customs and traditions. He appeared happier than ever before and wanted nothing more than to lavish Nikki with his charm and passion, although his growing need for heavier and heavier drugs may have worried some. And she didn't leave his side, as he stretched the limits of her cultural knowledge and pleasure. Nathan couldn't bear to watch, and spent his time with a few teenage boys exploring the indigenous wildlife, particularly the flightless kagu birds roaming the forest floor and numerous flying foxes hanging from trees.

By early evening, the gracious chief, Daoumi, blew a conch shell to call together a celebration for his guests. The youngest men built a roaring fire in the center of their semi-circular row of arrow-point huts. Then the young women presented a feast, with a main dish of bougna, a combination of chicken, seafood, yam, and taro wrapped in singed banana leaves. Nathan soaked in the atmosphere with every steaming bite. He could hardly grasp the incredible feeling of becoming a part of an ancient culture.

Later, a slender young woman walked up to Charge and handed him a dish of steaming roussette, explaining it was an island delicacy. After five or six big bites, he smiled, and with juice dripping down his face, inquired what it was. Every member of Billy's crew grew silent when the chief stood up and raised his arms for attention. With serious tone, he asked, "Big man, you like human flesh?" Charge stared at him in disbelief with his mouth open. Then the entire tribe burst into laughter when he spit out his last mouthful after the girl motioned to the trees, indicating that he was actually eating a flying fox.

When dinner ended, a few musicians came together to play for the gathering. A cluster of drums kept the beat growing while bamboo flutes and conch shells accentuated each other to create an atmosphere of enchantment. Young men donned with extravagant white and black body paint, and women dressed in bare-skinned ornaments, began to entertain the crew in the graceful art of Pilou. They performed a variety of dances telling stories of island life from ancient rituals, to family tragedies, to past battles. The trance-like state induced by the fervor and mystery of their moves was infectious. Shifting bodies held all eyes and commanding rhythms rang in the ears to make the experience more powerful than any drug trip. Nathan suddenly understood how such movement could lead to death strikes and the consumption of human flesh.

Their swirling silhouettes drew in Billy's wild spirit, and he stood up to join the commotion. Following the dancers' lead, he became a giant twister that twirled and twirled in the darkness. Things began to get out of control when he led the natives in wild leaps through the fire. At some point Nathan figured out that the dance was depicting devastating hurricanes from past years, and got his initial image of an ultimate surfing extreme, an idea that would soon rule his fate.

Feeling a bit charred and drained after the dance, Billy disappeared into the valley with a few of the young natives, apparently feeling the need to show them the joys of Western addiction. Six ebony girls were talking with their hands, telling the story of how New Caledonia had split from the mainland, when Nathan saw Nikki approach. She sat down by his side and said meekly, "Good even', Luv."

He replied in an irritated tone, "Hi Nikki, what brings you to my side of the fire?" It was the first time he'd spoken to her since that night of betrayal.

"You be nice." She looked up to the dancers and asked, "Can't get enough of this culture, know what I mean?"

"Yah, they make me feel like I'm one of them. But it's kind of scary though."

"I know. These dances give me the heebie-jeebies. But hey, listen Nathan, I've been wanting to apologize for a while now, but you've been very good at avoiding me. So, I'm sorry mate, I'm sorry if I hurt you back there."

Nathan just shook his head. And when she tried to explain why it happened, he stopped her mid sentence and told her to enjoy the night, because there was nothing like becoming a part of another way of life. He wondered what it would take for her to wake up and see the error in her ways, but outwardly he made it ok for her. The Pilou dancers were winding down their routine, although the fascinating music continued next to the flames. The chief dismissed his people and most of them wandered off into their various dwellings.

Nathan wouldn't admit just how much he was enjoying her presence, and Nikki couldn't understand just how much her company was tormenting him. As she got out a sack of weed and passed him her peace pipe, he wondered where Billy was. Nathan began to let down his guard and again imagined kissing her. Getting stoned together made the night more than perfect. They laughed and laughed, thighs rubbing together as they talked, and in time they seemed to breath as one. Finally, she grabbed his knee and said, "I like it when you take risks for me, why don't you sing me a song."

As he stared into her eyes, the wordless melodies carried his mind away; he grew lost in thought and meaning. Soon, Garo had picked up a bamboo flute and led the natives to a stray new melody. And that's when the energy again came together for Nathan, late that night, when he was wasted and fluid, unable to speak a clear sentence but incapable of holding in the creative uprising. With simultaneous force and gentle spirit that can only be found in the South Pacific, Nathan sang his own interpretation of the islands' lore. He sang to his pain, he sang to his heartache, but what came out echoed the simple elegance of the Kanak lifestyle. Speaking simultaneously of exotic ghosts in the night and complex societies of the future, he asked the world to find its peace, to quench its restless spirit. Those who were still awake began to sing along with tranquil voices, adding to the flawless night. When she squeezed his thigh with pleasure, he never felt so alive.

It was the moment he stopped taking life so seriously. He turned himself loose, letting go of inhibitions, worries, and the need to succeed. Life, death, inner, outer, success, failure, love, hate, none of it mattered any more. Life was a cruel joke, and Nathan decided to just have fun, open up, and let it ride. No more waiting, hoping, wishing. He pulled Nikki onto his lap, breathed deeply, and rested his chest on her shoulder blades, experiencing the moment with supreme clarity.

But Garo noticed his lack of boundaries and pulled him aside to have a word with him. While they walked over to the brush to take a piss, Garo warned, "You better be careful dude. I don't know what she's got on her mind, but Billy won't like it."

"Don't worry about us, we're just talking and laughing. Anyway, he must've passed out an hour ago because I haven't seen him since his fire dance."

"Yah, but I don't want him throwing you off the boat, so I'm gonna watch your back, bro."

"I appreciate it, but come on, he really doesn't care about Nikki."

"I don't know, he's been spending a lot of time with her."

"Whatever."

On the way back to the fire, they heard deep grunts coming from one of the outlying huts and decided to peak in to have a closer look at island life. Nathan's insecurities came rushing back when he saw one of the dark women who had greeted them earlier giving it to Billy island style.

Garo shook his head and whispered, "Ok man, you're right, he'll always be a dog."

Nathan only laughed and walked away. He wanted to tell Nikki what he'd seen, but was too disappointed to return to her. He knew even if he spilled his guts, things wouldn't change because they had a sick agreement of some kind. So he went to lie on the beach alone, seething as he thought about Billy's bare-ass streaked with black tribal paint pumping in the night. He couldn't understand why his friend was allowed to carry on with his lifestyle, running over anything in his way, imposing his will on people for pure pleasure. And as he dozed into an uneasy sleep, Nathan knew once and for all that life was too short to live; he needed to burn.

He was stirred awake the next morning by the sound of a single engine plane landing in the lagoon next to him, apparently dropping off food and medical supplies to the islanders. Remembering the attention he'd received from his nighttime glow session, Nathan knew immediately what he wanted to do. He met the eccentric pilot, a shriveled man from years of too much sun, at the platform of the pontoon, and asked if he needed help unloading supplies.

Within an hour, he'd talked 'Raisin' into taking him for a breath-taking ride on his plane. Nathan strapped a surfboard to his ankles, clipped a rope on his lifejacket, and tied it to the back of the plane. As he sat in the shallows with his old and new friends watching, he signaled to "Go for it."

The plane began moving forward, preparing for take off, dragging him through the shallow water face-first and sideways. When the craft built up enough speed to lift off, Nathan planed out and rose to his feet like an acrobatic water skier. And by the time the low-lying aircraft had looped around and headed back past the beach, Nathan was virtually flying, slaloming from side to side with reckless abandon. But as the plane gained speed and altitude, he found himself skipping across the ocean like a stone, jumping waves at over a hundred miles an hour, hanging on air like he never imagined. Raisin couldn't see behind him so when Nathan's board cracked in half and he ate it, the plane kept right on flying. Nathan became a human avalanche of ocean spray, board foam, and body parts tumbling along the water's surface.

He finally cut himself free with the safety knife he kept in his board shorts, and came to rest in the calm morning sea. While he was carted back to the beach on the pontoon, the inhabitants welcomed him with cheers. Although he suffered bruised ribs and a bloody nose, he was full of life, gaining insatiable attention from the reckless feat. Nikki pulled him aside later and asked how far he'd go to have a good time. He smiled and said, "I don't know, guess you're gonna have to watch me."

Throughout most of February, March, and April of 1991, the magnificent ship faded from reality in the midst of the eighty plus islands of Vanuatu. Gradually, while high on top of his post reflecting on the ebb and flow of endless ocean currents, Nathan became aware of the repetitive maze that was his life. It's true, the surfer lifestyle can close you in, limiting your view and turning existence into a looping cycle of adrenaline. But for him, the flashing days and blurred nights were duplicate photos of exhilaration and excess, freeing him from the pages of time.

His reality became an intricate mix of bold dares, cultural entropy, crazy rides, and creative expression. When the surf was pumping, entire songs poured through his head while alone in a hollow tube. When it wasn't big, he'd try his luck at other wild stunts like rock climbing, spear fishing, or hang gliding, anything to find that rush. One evening the ship passed the summit of the Yasur Volcano, and he ordered Kerby to drop anchor right there. He then climbed partway up the active volcano, stood at the edge of a vent and watched glowing lava spill into the sea, its energy mirroring the passion in his heart.

A few days later, after noticing a hundred foot rock face sticking out of the jungle of another deserted isle, he forced the ship to pause once again. He spent the entire afternoon hiking up to the summit, and with the chute he had bought off of Raisin, discovered his passion for base-jumping. And as he dropped through narrow walls, inches from the jagged rock, entire albums streamed from his soul.

Those months were the wildest of his life, and even the legendary Captain Kerby was at a loss for words after witnessing some of his extreme feats. Each night, Nathan indulged a bit more in the hard drugs, island culture, loose women, and endless songs that were suddenly so easy to find. Nighttime jam sessions became elaborate showcases for his new style, resembling full concerts rather than fireside chants. For days at a time, he'd dive into his multi-layered brilliance, tapping into wave after wave of focused freedom. The guys would sometimes look at each other in disbelief while playing, as Nathan so often left them behind. As everyone swayed together in unison, having the time of their lives, he'd mix it up, tease the island women shaking their shakers or tapping their bongos, and come out the other end with a unique perspective and new strength. With eyes closed, emotions open, he was living the dream. Everyone felt like a part of it, but in reality, he was playing for her. Secretly, he only played for Nikki. And as his music progressed to new levels of genius, no one understood how much he was still hurting.

If someone would have videoed those first shows, they would have captured some of the most powerful moments in musical history. The melodies and lyrics changed from night to night; they were so far reaching that Nathan stopped trying to write them down. But complete songs were sometimes captured in early morning recordings. Thirty or forty songs were recorded in all, along with parts of hundreds more. Many years later, the missing tapes would blow the lid off the intimacy of those early sessions.

But there was a price to pay for continuously burning the candle and both ends. Nathan's recall of the time, increasingly known by the crew as the 'wildfire sessions,' was nothing more than distorted movements of chaos. One morning, after staying up

72

virtually eight nights in a row, he forced himself to go back to the boat alone after vomiting in the forest for over an hour. He had gulped cups of *kava* for several nights in a row, and the mixture of chewed leaves squeezed into a liquid narcotic finally pushed him over the edge. Scattered memories resurfaced, haunting him with wicked visions. Reality and fantasy blurred with new form and he wondered if he had really hunted pigs with spears or wore distorted masks while running through dense forests.

While lying on the deck of the ship with no one else around, his ears began to ring and his mind began to break down. A tattoo he'd gotten on his forearm from a chief's favorite artist started moving around and speaking to him. At that point, he wondered, *can I really speak Bislama?* Hundreds of faces from isolated cultures swirled to the center of his thoughts, speaking countless words from strange languages. Strange rituals and recurring ceremonies came to light, the partial memories of past evenings finding fresh life. A mask lying beside Nathan began to sing to him about his women, Gabriel, Heather, Jenny, Caitlin, and all the local girls he'd been with. Suddenly he remembered the morning a few nights back when he woke up lying with Billy and Nikki.

By this time, he was hanging over the bow, heaving out his dry guts. After rolling over and looking up at a gentle cloud breezing by in the sky, he tried to force himself to breath. He attempted to think clearly. *Heavy, heavy drugs. Too heavy. Good times, fried minds.* But he just couldn't keep his thoughts. *Ritualistic chants. Share their Kava. Share their women. Share their contempt. Are they laughing at me as they share her thigh?*

73

Shadows of people he cared for were spinning around the sky while he remained stationary on the floor of the deck. They were talking to him behind his ears, singing him one of his songs, only with odd new words. *Beating Billy. Beating women? Eating pig. Eating man?* Issues of every kind found their way in and out, childhood memories merging with universal questions and scientific fiction finding humor in his disbelief. *A woman's trust, my own desire, the nature of affection, the importance of reflection.* One idea kept resurfacing, the strange relationship that was unfolding between Billy, Nikki, and himself. He began to scream, desperately calling for it all to go away.

He knew he needed to get away from this life or he'd do something crazy, something final. He crawled halfway down the stairs towards his room, hearing Billy's radio in the distance, an Australian woman speaking softly about the week's weather forecast. He was able to use this distraction as a focal point to disperse the visions, and finally eased himself into a nervous sleep.

He slept for a day and a half, giving his brain a chance to let go of the intensity. In an endless dream, he hopelessly chased Nikki through murky water and swirling air, her hands and feet just out of his reach. All the while, he knew at a semi-conscious level he was burning out from the inside. When he finally awoke, the only thing he remembered about the experience was the weather report coming in from the north Indian Ocean. With fresh determination, he went directly to Billy with news of his decision.

6.

Nathan grew fixated on stories of daredevils who surfed massive storm surges, and was itching at a chance to add a similar experience to his resume of self-destruction. Billy didn't believe the opportunity would ever arise, but agreed to fund a trip out of amusement for Nathan's intentions. So on the morning of April 27th, 1991, Billy, Nathan, Charge, and Nikki boarded a small plane from the island of Efate, Vanuatu, headed to Bangkok, Thailand, and then hooked up with a commercial flight taking them to the port city of Chittagong, Bangladesh. While on the plane, they learned the storm approaching the Bay of Bengal had already achieved extreme intensity, although it was still days from landfall.

Upon arrival to Southern Asia, the crew hired a decrepit little man to take them by rickshaw to the most lavish district in search of lodging. With anticipation of the ultimate ride playing havoc on his insides, Nathan suggested they take some time to explore the sites. He was expecting a cultural shock, a third world nation struggling to feed its people, but was surprised at how clean, orderly, and well kept the central city was. Located in the foothills of the Himalayas, the heart of Chittagong looked more like a living anthropological site than a decaying city. While walking the most significant sections of town, Nathan took in every detail of the intricate buildings, geometrical mosques, and elaborate palaces dotting the sections on higher ground. And he might as well have been walking on air as he listened to his friends' nervous chatter about the approaching storm.

75

When Billy complained that his feet were hurting, he flagged down a local merchant and bargained to lease an auto-rickshaw. The crew spent the rest of the day cruising to various points of interest including the Dargah Shrine and the remains of an ancient military fort known as the Andar Killa. When evening approached, they reached the top of a picturesque knoll known as Fairy Hill. There, Billy rented a luxurious bungalow to act as headquarters for the duration of their stay. From the exquisite balcony, Nikki made a mental note of the modern hospital facing them from lower ground towards the sea. Then Nathan pointed to the Karnaphuli River emptying into the Bay of Bengal and wondered why fishing boats were still departing from the port at the river mouth. Looking out at the scene like a Persian lord, Billy toasted his wine glass to the peasants entering the throat of the storm and the foursome felt a peculiar connection with one another. But Nathan fell out of the moment when he caught a glimpse of Nikki whispering in Billy's ear.

At sunrise the next morning, they discovered that the ocean remained a sheet of glass, not worth going out to try to find a break. So they made their way down to the port to reserve a reliable boat and inquire about the best big breaks. Along the way, Billy and the crew saw more and more of how the other half lived. While walking the filthy flats running along the coast, he laughed at the tiny stone dwellings with corrugated roofs housing thousands of underprivileged individuals. He was the first to notice that despite the wicked forecast, things were generally business-as-usual for the locals. Some families were packing up their bullock carts to evacuate, but most seemed to scoff at the warnings and carry on with their simple lives. Billy was losing his patience and questioned out loud whether the people there were simply ignorant or if the forecast was a false alarm.

Nathan tried to ignore his companion to enjoy the strange new society and the build-up he was experiencing inside. He knew without doubt the Bengali existence was a stark contrast to island living, as endless customs had melded together to form a unique culture of its own. He observed the Muslims as they stopped five times a day to pray in the heart of the city, and the strange music calling them together in orderly intervals kept bringing to mind Hemingway's *For Whom the Bell Tolls*. Feeling the first hints of cultural shock, he began to wonder if he even believed in God any more. Yet, he remained low key, almost meditative, silently preparing for a challenge the others could not conceive. As the day wore on, he knew, if nothing else, it was a good opportunity to dry out and get a clear mindset.

The Bengalis were generally friendly and curious, many making attempts to interact with them as they mingled in the public marketplace. Nikki grew captivated by a particular boy who stood on one leg in the middle of the crowd. He caught a glimpse of her smile and followed her for more than a half hour, repeatedly performing simple magic tricks, games of chance, and juggling acts, before finally asking for a handout. Billy may have felt a twinge of his concealed cruelty as he insisted that the boy trade one of his homemade trinkets for a few worthless coins.

Sensing the power he possessed over the feeble, Billy became enthralled with bartering with the local Chittagonians and Nikki began to feel like an Arabian princess from all the jewelry she was offered. Even more, she was falling in love with the beautiful people and their fascinating ways, and aimed to soak up as much of their culture as time would allow. But her experience was cut short when Charge asked to test out the local nightlife, and the group voted to return to their bungalow because of rumors of brutal acts of terrorism performed on tourists at night.

By the morning of April 29th, the storm had reached the strength of a Category 5 Hurricane, although the water along the coast remained surprisingly calm. But the forecasters insisted the big one would hit at any time. Billy had chartered an old thirty-foot fishing boat named *Aro*, which quite fittingly means 'More' in Bengali. He had chosen the vessel with the most powerful engine to ensure they could get through the strongest surge. By nine o'clock, they had loaded the weathered craft with supplies and were off in search of a strong break point.

The first sign of a change in local custom came as they left the port and passed dozens of narrow fishing boats rushing for the security of land. Theirs was the only boat heading out to sea, and the friends began to understand the impending risk. The typical light mood filled with wise cracks and easy conversation began to shift to a somber focus on the task at hand.

The afternoon sky was a picture-perfect blue, but an eerie calm sat on the horizon; the surreal feeling filled their minds with anxiety and excitement. Billy had committed to driving the craft through the greater part of the storm while Nikki was along to take photographs, which left Nathan and Charge to try their luck on the unfamiliar waves. Billy's plan was to allow the two to surf as long as they could and then race for shore as soon as the wind and waves were too much for them to safely maneuver.

Through the early part of the day there was no swell. Billy grew impatient and again questioned whether the storm would ever hit. But towards late afternoon, a swirling wall of devastation grew visible in the distance. The horizon was turning a dismal black and the mountainous clouds made Nikki shudder. Gradually, the waves built in size and strength and Billy found a good break about a half-mile out that was releasing consistent eight-foot rollers.

Before tempting fate, Billy stopped the guys and made one of his patented speeches. He stood on the bow, pointed to the deep and said, "The only thing we can count on right now is that a strong storm surge is about as unpredictable as a rabid rat. I know the two of you want to be heroes and all, but I want to see your ugly mugs again. So I brought these to help spot you in the surge. Now put them on." Nathan and Charge balked at first, but after witnessing fluid changes in the pattern of the waves less than a minute later, they put the life jackets on without complaint. Then they jumped into the churning ocean, geared for the ultimate test.

As they paddled into indefinite peril with adrenaline rollicking down their spines, violent gusts and pelting showers hit them with metal-like intensity. Nathan's senses turned keenly aware, taking in the sights and sounds of his bizarre setting. The

79

inky black surge swirling with crests of mercury silver was daunting, intimidating. And the streaks of yellow sunlight shooting through the black sky made him feel like he had entered a liquid war zone.

But surfing cyclone size waves was everything Nathan hoped it would be. For over two hours, the weather steadily declined while the waves grew larger and more powerful. The random break points made every wave a contest, every ride a fierce test of skill and nerve. And Nathan was up to every challenge as the size increased from ten, to fifteen, to twenty feet. Seizing his flair for the dramatic, it was the finest he surfed in his life. In fact, the harder the wind blew and the faster the waves broke, the more he seemed to lock into an extraordinary zone. He felt so small in the face of Mother Nature, so insignificant, making him feel all the more invincible. It's hard to put into words just how spectacular a picture he was painting with his sharp bursts of speed and raining blasts of spray in the face of liquid demolition, the last frontier of man conquering beast.

When a gust of wind drove Charge off his board at the top of a twenty-five foot crest, he was blown through the air like a broken kite, flying end over end until he finally crashed into the base of the next wave. The awkward entry caused him to churn helplessly underwater for too long, and it took all he had to fight through the relentless undertow to the surface. He finally had had enough, and motioned to the boat to pick him up.

Billy, trying to spot the surfers from just outside the break zone, was having his own trouble keeping the boat stable. He motioned to Nathan to call it quits, but Nathan was in a world of his own, plunging through an impossibly steep section that was exploding with brownish foam. Ninety mile-per-hour winds were blowing the rain sideways and Nathan had to hang on to his rails just to keep his footing. As Charge climbed up the rickety ladder, he looked back and shouted, "Look at that kid, he's chargin' harder than I do."

But after narrowly escaping the impact zone, Nathan knew he was pushing his luck, and gestured that he was going to catch just one more wave. Seabirds were floating face down all around him and he shook his head in disbelief when a red-necked stint slashed past his shoulder and went into the sea like a living torpedo. Various pieces of debris were gathering in the surrounding mishmash, and he could only sigh when a spiked plank flew directly over his head. Then, as he paddled towards the next open face, the bow of a broken-up fishing boat tumbled over the top of the wave and sideswiped his upper body. These murky omens told him it was time to find safety, yet his ego just wouldn't let him get out unscathed. He heard Nikki's terrified calls through his blood-streaked face, impelling him to keep searching for that elusive last wave. After all, he was the center of attention in the face of God, and felt that the others would only accept him if he outdid them all.

It was a critical point in his life, the moment when the tone changed from dangerous challenge to senseless threat. Billy could no longer keep control of the boat as thick mounds of brown water dumped over the starboard side with increasing regularity. He was incredibly cool under pressure but knew they were on the verge of capsizing. Nikki grew so scared that she went down below and hid in the tiny cabin. Charge was holding onto a thick wooden handrail at the stern, waving to Nathan to come in. But the danger-boy continued to paddle with his head down, repeating to himself how important it was to catch that ultimate wave.

By the time Nathan glanced back to gauge his next point of entry, it was too late. A massive set rolled in with the sound of death, like a liquid serpent honing in on her prey. Nathan saw her forty-foot face thicker than a concrete barricade heading at him. He had no other choice but to paddle forward, hoping she would hold up until he made it over the top. But her lines were breaking well beyond the horizon, so he knew right then he was as good as dead.

Two-thirds of the way up, the arching angel smiled down upon him from her apex--he could do nothing but brace for impact. Plummeting backwards thirty feet with the break, the hollow monster exploded into him with a thousand watery sledgehammers. His only thought was that he had never been hit so hard in his life-- there was instant darkness and pain. The air was forced out of his lungs and he was left gulping the ocean's bitter water. There can be no worse feeling than knowing you're going down into the depths of the abyss with no breath.

For a moment he thought the relentless power from above would never let him go. But he paddled with all he had, struggling to break free from her grip. Ten, twelve, fifteen strokes, straight up. And just after he broke the surface, another cascade crushed him, halting his progress for survival. Her supremacy was immediate, absolute. He felt himself rolling into the depths, twisting out of control, and when his leash wrapped around both legs, he grew calm with the realization that he was drowning. Her black blanket of blue enveloped him and made him quiver with a fear from another world. Water poured down his throat, yet still he fought to stay in control, to hold on—and just as he began to gain hope, he saw the biggest wave of the set rolling towards him. He cursed Mother Nature's brutal power, her merciless ways, although it was those same challenges that he loved in her. Unable to handle another round, he was forced to dive the depths in order to lighten the impact. He must have been fifteen feet under when he felt her blast take him down once more. He rolled and twisted seven or eight times as her undertow sucked him into her belly. By the time he came to his senses, he was suffering from vertigo and unsure which way was up.

Paddling with all he had, his hand reached for the surface and hit something hard and spiky. Coral! He'd been swimming in the wrong direction. His mind exploded with a lack of oxygen and his last desperate option was to curl up and spring as hard as he could for the surface. As he jetted up, he began to accept the burning sensation of saltwater streaming into his lungs.

Nearly unconscious, he broke through and felt the swirling wind whipping his face. With eyes closed, he held onto his splintered board, foamy vomit seeping from his mouth and nose. For the first time in years, he prayed to a higher power to free him from her clutches. Instead, he heard more massive waves in the distance, like Nazi Stukas with their ugly sirens blaring, preparing him for a bombing raid. Out of strength and breath, he bobbed up and down waiting for the attack to curl over him. She struck quick and hard and he was tossed in a thousand directions at once. He felt his leash rip from his ankle, and as he was whisked away from his board like a rag doll, he knew he had no fight left in him. When the top of his head collided with a solid object from above, the darkness began to blend with the light.

At the surface, Cyclone 2B was hitting the dark coast with the force of a nuclear explosion, and it was too late for *Aro* to escape. For a while, Billy had done an incredible job fighting through the waves, but he lost the battle when a breaker engulfed the stern and flooded the engine compartment. The engine quit, and they were now at the mercy of the storm. Nikki climbed to the bridge to gain a sense of security from Billy, but lost it when she realized Nathan was nowhere to be found. Charge was fiddling with the motor, and Nikki inched her way over to him to seek some help. He ignored her at first, so she pounded on his back and screamed in incoherent bursts, "Help me find him, you bloody asshole! Don't you see he's out there because of me?"

"There's nothing I can do, I can barley hold on."

"But he's not gonna make it."

" Nikki, if I don't get this engine runnin', *we're* not gonna make it."

"Then I'm going in after him."

She pulled herself up in the teeth of the wind and began to climb over the rail. Charge had to rip her from the top wrung and tackle her on the sloping, flooded deck. He held her there while the listless boat continued to wash around like a leaf in a gushing stream. Billy systematically turned the engine over again and again, and a few times came close to working his magic and sparking life back into their only means of survival. But the relentless waves continued

84

to pound them into submission, and at some point they got stuck in the falls of an exploding right and began to wash sideways down the line.

Nikki clung to a cracked fishing mount at the stern, wailing at the churning sea, when she spotted a yellow smudge tossing and turning in the whitewash two hundred yards to the west. Nathan was somehow caught in the same eddy as them, and in the one miracle of the day, his limp body was skipping along directly towards them. It was then that Nikki made a secret promise to herself to change her ways if they succeeded in reaching him.

She screamed to Charge through the deafening gales, begging him to help get Nathan. He made his way to a rigging box, tied a rope around his waist, secured himself to the rail, and waited for the right moment. He dove in when Nathan's body changed directions less than twenty yards from their craft. Charge swam through the swirling ruins like a champion, and just as he reached his target he ran out of slack in the rope. He saw Nathan's head face down in the dark water and knew he had only a few more seconds before his friend would wash away forever. The big man reached with every tendon of his long wingspan, extending his fingers until his nerve endings burned with agony, and caught the loop of the life jacket with the tip of his middle finger. He pulled Nathan's body into his and waved at the boat to get them in.

Billy and Nikki worked together to drag the heavy load on board. As Charge struggled to help them get Nathan onto the deck, he couldn't help thinking of what he'd said to him that night he'd pulled him out of the drink the second time. Finally, Nathan was rolled up and over the railing. He landed on top of Nikki and she fell back onto her bum. While his weight pinned her to the floor, she sighed deeply with eternal relief and began hugging and kissing him all over his head and neck. But he didn't respond to her warmth, and she looked into his face and realized he wasn't breathing.

## 7.

Nathan's glassy eyes stared wide open to the black hells of heaven, while massive raindrops continuously baptized his blank face. Nikki could no longer contain her feeling of helplessness, and pounded on his body with self-imposed desperation. She called to Billy, she called to the storm, she called to the gods, pleading with anyone to help the boy breath. The vessel washed towards the vanishing shoreline and Charge crawled over to them. He straddled his friend's midsection, ripped open the life jacket, and began compressing his chest with quick thrusts.

The surge along the water's edge engulfed them like a vicious scavenger attacking an unguarded nest. The shallows and beaches had turned into a vortex of swirling sludge, sucking thatched bamboo, palm branches, and crumbled billboards in crisscrossing directions with the force of a burst damn. The boat washed over a break wall protecting the shore, over low-lying shrubbery lining the beach, and began slamming through market stands and crumbling walls, unremittingly following the flow inland. As they were swept down a sloping alley that quickly became the main waterway entering the city, the keel got caught on a mound of sunken cars, twisted rickshaws, and floating bodies trapped at the entrance to a wider street.

When the next surge swelled over the narrow passage, the stern swung around, caught the back wall of the alleyway, and they tipped towards the rushing current. Water poured over the boat, and for a few moments they were completely submerged. Charge was swept off the deck, but reached back and grabbed the railing just as he went overboard. Nikki squeezed Nathan around the armpits, lodged her toes and elbows in the cracked wooden deck and held on. She watched as coolers and surfboards tied down along the starboard side were ripped from the planks and sent floating away in the city of sea. But as soon as the force of the suction cleared, Nikki lifted Nathan's body from the flooded deck, placed him on the wooden compartment encasing the engine, and went right back to working on him.

Nathan's skin was a drained white, his nostrils dripping water, but his expression was peaceful. Nikki tried to ignore the sound of cracking ribs and ripping tendons as she pumped his breastplate with all she had. She stared down at him while blowing two mouthfuls of air into his lungs, noticing his slightly upturned face, his matted hair, the shark tooth necklace hanging from his neck, the ripped rash guard covering his chest, and started quivering with silent sobs. Slow, cruel reality began to sink in. He wasn't moving. He wasn't breathing. He had no pulse. She had no idea how long he'd bobbed face down in the water like a dead albatross. Very soon he'd be lost forever; maybe he was already gone.

And the storm was making sure that help wasn't on the way. Cyclone 2B had no feminine name, no romantic title, but her power was unrivaled in the long history of tropical storms. More frightening, her most intense hours were upon them, as the whorl of her eye wall ripped through everything in her path. Down the coast in the ship breaking yards, half dismantled hulks of giant freighters were being tossed around with playful ease, grating and pounding together like massive Lego blocks clashing with steel dinosaurs. Further east, a 100-ton crane was ripped from its base and collapsed on the Karnaphuli River Bridge, turning both moonlights to steel carnage. And on the coastal air base, countless airplanes from the Bangladesh Air Force were being thrown around like toys, many landing on crumbling rooftops or in sheared trees.

All around, curved boats of every size were breaking through docks, trees, and shacks, or breaking up on stone slabs, rock walls, and concrete buildings. The wind wailed at 150 miles per hour, whipping the foliage and launching limbs like spears through wooden planks, including the side of the hull. Billy, who had given up on the engine in attempt to get the bilge pump running, was forced to edge over to Charge to give him a hand. As he pulled him in, a heavy electrical pole came down hard on the bow, and the stern was lifted out of the water at a forty-five degree angle. The two guys were forced to give up any chance at future safety in order to save their immediate lives. Charge did his best to pry the splintered stern from the tight trap of the wall, while Billy used a wooden oar to keep the sparking hot wires elevated, narrowly avoiding the snaking line from making contact with him. All the while, the surge continued to rise and fall over the hull in long, sweeping torrents.

Nikki, left to fend for herself, was experiencing an absolute loss of control. The sites and sounds became magnified, as if they were taking place inside her, racking her brain with vibrant anxiety. Glass shattering, shards flying. Eves creaking, supports giving way. Power lines crackling, blue flames sizzling. Voices calling. Dogs yelping. Children gurgling. She couldn't take it anymore, but there was nothing to do but focus on *fifteen and two*, look into Nathan's eyes and pray she would see a spark of life. Almost robotically, she remained alert and kept working on him long after she knew it was too late. But it was no use; she was helpless, powerless, tiny, so very tiny.

As she leaned over to release another breath into his mouth, she glanced through the broken deck railing and saw a large rat with beady pink eyes staring back at her from atop a broken doorframe. Billy's speech flashed through her mind and she knew in that moment that they were no better off than the pathetic little creature. She understood that in the eyes of God, they had no more right to live than a flea clinging to the bugger's saturated tail. Nikki looked into the fiercest curvature of the clouds and screamed for a bloody end to it all. A calm set in on her as she prepared to lift up Nathan's sprawling body and jump overboard, ready to join him in his peaceful rest.

But hope came bursting back when she blew a final breath into his mouth and he let out a single wheezing cough and a gallon of seawater spurted from his lungs. She quickly checked his vitals and told herself he had regained a faint pulse, although it was clear he still wasn't breathing on his own. The glimmer of life filled her nerves with motion, but just as quickly a new rush of fear entered her mind. He had been without air for too long, so even if he made it there was the possibility of brain damage.

A second blast of optimism came from the storm itself when the exploding wind smacked the building they were wedged between squarely in the chops. The far section of it gave way, crumbling into the underwater abyss, and suddenly they were free. The two men concentrated on dumping out the bricks and debris caught in the stern and then Billy further stabilized the situation when he got the pumps running.

While riding the massive surge three quarters of a mile inland, floating death and frenzied life were all around. The desperate silhouettes waving to them from the tops of caving roofs made them shiver with remorse, but their immediate end was to keep the boat afloat. They were utterly out of control and unable to attempt rescue on the endless children, elderly, and animals floating down the streets. More than once, Nikki saw individuals frantically trying to keep their heads above water, wretched expressions pleading for help, round eyes calling for air, clutched fingers reaching for broken branches. An old man with a toothless grimace was run down by the bow and Nikki looked back to see if he would resurface, but he was gone forever. Some of the victims saw her, but there was little she could do except reach a hand out to them to show how much she was hurting for them, and die a little more inside her soul.

After navigating wild rapids down granite staircases and through the ruins of an elaborate mosque, the tide began to wane and the boat changed directions, sweeping back towards the ocean. Their path was altered when they were sucked into a narrow cascade passing through a series of lush hills in the middle of town. The rushing rivulet took them for a ride through the thicket until they finally got lodged on a series of curling limbs and twisted trunks along the base of a knoll.

Having made landfall, the three of them were able to focus entirely on Nathan's resuscitation. Foremost, they needed to get him out of the drenching rain as water was pouring into his mouth and down his throat. Because the cabin was flooded, Billy and Charge ripped out a few of the benches and built him a makeshift shelter in the corner under the gunwale. Nikki continued to provide him with oxygen every three seconds until she grew faint from exhaustion. Her relief came out in blissful cries, as she shouted, "Holy Jesus, did ya see that? He sucked in some air. Boys, he took a breath." She continued to monitor his rising chest and give him occasional breaths until it was obvious that he was doing it on his own. She tried to talk to him to get him to come around, but he remained unresponsive.

They sat silently waiting to meet their fate as the boat continued to disintegrate all around them. The upper deck swayed and creaked back and forth and eventually there was an earsplitting crack. The entire bridge was ripped from its supports and collapsed on deck, sending jagged splinters in every direction, including a nine-inch piece of fiberglass that stuck into Charge's back. He reached back and yanked it out with not so much as a grunt.

Billy made the decision to abandon the *Aro* once and for all. Nikki helped him lift Nathan over the crushed gunwale and they lowered him to Charge who was standing in chest deep water. Billy pulled out the high beam flashlight from the emergency box and they set out in search of help.

However, the storm was still too powerful for open eyes, let alone movement. After a few moments fighting the impossible wind, they scrambled up the side of the hill to look for cover. They found a sloping slab of rock protruding from the foliage and squeezed their way in to hide. There, they were pinned for most of the night, crammed together like a nest of miserable rodents. Amid howling gusts of wind and booming thunder, they heard repeated cries for help that would never come.

For the first time since meeting each other, neither Billy nor Charge could come up with a witty wisecrack to lighten the mood. The two of them had grown exhausted from their heroic actions and slowly faded into an uncomfortable slumber. But Nikki couldn't let go of the voices, for she felt as insignificant as the millions of peons washing away with the land, as irrelevant as a statistic in one of her useless history books. She could only listen to the disturbing sounds and look at the miracle she'd helped create. The shallow rise and fall of his chest kept her going through the night. As long as he had one more breath to give, she wouldn't lose control. As long as she could monitor his weak pulse, she was glad to be right there in the dirty old cave so far from her beautiful mare Yonkers and the comforting sounds of home.

But late that night Nathan took a turn for the worse. His skin grew pallid and his breaths weak. There was a moment when he stopped breathing again and Nikki had to force-feed him air in order to keep him alive. She woke up the guys, pleading for help, but there was little they could do except check his vitals and confirm that he was declining. Nikki stared out of the crack in the cave watching the pounding rain, knowing in her heart that he was dying right in front of her. For a time, she dozed into a trance-like gaze, but she was yanked out of it by the silence of Nathan's soul. She grew so desperate that she demanded they leave immediately, no matter the consequences.

As they piled out of their gritty shelter, lady luck suddenly turned to their side. Just before dawn, Cyclone 2B began to loosen her grip on the tired city of Chittagong. Minutes after they left, the sun's rays burst through the sky with such beauty that it seemed as if they were being given a gift from heaven. All around were the giant, curving black clouds, but right overhead was a vivid blue sky streaked with the colors of a magnificent sunset. They were in the eye of the storm, and as the wind died to a gentle breeze, an unnerving calm settled upon the disabled city.

Their spirits were stirred when they saw Fairy Hill over the next rise, and Nikki remembered the hospital they'd passed on the way to the bungalow. Inch by inch, they made their way over the higher ground. But when they began their descent down the other side, the reality of the devastation grew evident. Tin shacks crushed like flattened cans, ancient footbridges washed away without a trace, twisted roofs piled on each other like trash. A magnificently sculpted stone building stood alone in their path, relatively unharmed, but buried in the ruins. They passed a splendid fountain that had recently been the center of a garden, and Billy had to sigh when he saw the streams shooting sideways with a brownish orange slush. It reminded him of Caesar's bloody statue in Calpurnia's dream.

They carried Nathan's limp body silently over the saturated land. Bloated corpses of every genus littered the muddy ground. Chickens. Goats. Horses. People. Most of the humans were sprawled nude in graceless positions, their clothes ripped off by the surge. Such a humiliating way to come to your final rest. Imagine what the spirits leaving their mangled bodies must have thought as they looked down on their own disgrace. Worst were the channels of rushing sludge, raw sewage of death draining down the streets with half submerged human bodies tumbling alongside hogs, baskets, tires, and cows. Liquid holocaust.

As they crossed a backwashing stream, a bloated woman with nothing on but a homemade burka bumped against Billy's thigh. He kicked her out of disgust and she continued on her way, floating face down with the current. But his action made the others aware of the living. Suddenly, blank stares and helpless gazes met the crew from every angle. Survivors were beginning to stir from the thousands of pools of water draining into the sea, most standing and watching, paralyzed with shock. Some were simply lying in the mud, waiting for help to arrive, their purple skin and sunken chests highlighting internal wounds. Lost eyes told stories of denial, doubt, terror, for they had just lost a one-sided battle with Allah.

Nikki stopped to help an incoherent mother who was searching through the water for her child, but Billy forced her to press on, reminding her of their obligation to Nathan. After nearly twenty-four hours of sleepless misery, she was losing touch with her ability to think clearly. To make matters worse, the sky was once again growing dark with each tired step. By the time they reached the top of Fairy Hill, the backside of the storm was upon them. Crisp gusts of wind awoke the fear in the city, tossing around rubble that had already been set loose. The crew ran the final two hundred yards to the hospital as the skies opened with torrents of rain and crackling bolts of lightening.

The hospital had suffered severe structural damage to the roof and south wing, but remained frantically operational. Hundreds of individuals were milling around in chaotic despair. There was no chance of waiting through the bedlam to seek help for Nathan, so Billy used the only thing that had ever worked for him, his money. He spotted a young doctor working haphazardly on two patients in the middle of the hallway, drifted over to him and whispered something in his ear. Moments later, Dr. Faizabad accepted a wad of American cash in exchange for a quick look at his friend. The thin man slipped away from his post and led Billy to a small room full of somewhat modern equipment. There, after a crash course training session, the two of them worked to hook Nathan up to the last remaining breathing machine in the area.

Charge took Nikki to what remained of the waiting room. With little choice, the staff had turned it into a makeshift morgue as dozens of dead bodies littered the floor. But what she saw on the other side of the room changed her perspective even more. Leaning against the wall in the far corner was Uzzal, the one-legged boy from the market holding the drowned carcass of his infant brother. He had apparently held onto to him throughout the strongest forces of the undertow, but just couldn't keep his brother's head above water as he struggled to save his own life. Nikki went to him with open arms, but the kid stared right through her, unable to recognize human contact, tightening his grip on his brother as she tried to relieve him of his burden. She promised herself right then that she wouldn't leave the devastated country until she helped make things right. As she tried in vain to break through to the boy, her only comfort was in the idea that she'd led the charge to get Nathan the care he needed.

She was kneeling over, holding the exhausted boy in her arms when Billy appeared in front of her less than an hour later. Looking past her, he tried to make everything ok. But her eyes grew a few shades darker and more focused as he prepared the news with his charming reassurance. Finally, she reached up, yanked his head around to face her eye to eye, and said, "Cut through the chase ya slimy chook, how's he doing?"

Leaning over to her ear, he whispered, "He looks peaceful enough to me. He's hooked up to a breathing machine and seems pretty stable."

"Oh yah mate, then why you being so bloody dodgy?"

"Nikki, the doctor doesn't know for sure what's wrong," he hesitated, but then let it out, "but he appears to be in a coma."

Nikki fell backwards to the floor with the little boy still in her arms, exhaustion, emotion, and fear at last getting the best of her.

96

8.

The crew spent the next day crammed in a narrow hallway alternating between bouts of restless sleep and hours of crouching by Nathan's side. They were weathered and shaken, showing post-traumatic effects through their strange and erratic behaviors. For a time, Billy sought to pay off other doctors and nurses, but after limited success in gaining a miracle cure, he began to distance himself from the aftermath. As his body recovered from exhaustion, a spark in his eye foreshadowed his intention of running from the whole scene. Charge, on the other hand, was getting involved in the recovery efforts with the ardor of a cranky ogre, pushing feeble men out of line in the scramble for relief supplies and swearing at the top of his lungs when he couldn't get enough food packets. But what upset him more than the harsh truth was the fact that he was fiending for a drink in a country that practiced strict prohibition. By early afternoon, he'd scavenged a case of Bangla Mad from the handcart of an underground brewer, and after pounding a few bottles of the strange brew he was more or less himself again.

Nikki was the worst off of the three, edging in and out of hallowed places in her mind, perhaps wishing to visit Nathan's quiet world. After hours of staring at his motionless eyes with nothing to do to help, she got up and walked out of the hospital to offer her services to the thousands of victims milling around. Having little knowledge of the language or social order, she didn't know where to begin and quickly grew overwhelmed by the ghastly realities. She left the grounds and wandered past hundreds of town folk digging through saturated rubble, watching the commotion with tears raining down her cheeks. A few times she offered assistance to a weeping grandmother or a panicked widow, but was met with nothing but strange stares and angry curses.

So Nikki was driven towards the deserted coastline to get her mind together. As she made her way towards the coffee stained sea, she noticed that the citizens were focusing their energies on helping the walking wounded, which meant that most of the dead bodies were still lying in their final places of rest. While passing deformed manikins one after another, she thought long and hard, staring at the lifeless shells caked in mud, crusted with gunk, each in the midst of a legitimate life just yesterday. She was on the verge of a break down, as a worming torment tunneled through her spirit and ate her up from the inside. Why had she left her mum and pop's ranch? For fun. Freedom. Adventure. It had all gone wrong. Guilt, sadness, and shame were all that remained.

She sat on a twisted stump gazing out at the unruly Bay of Bengal, and suddenly a fresh resilience began to bubble up from her depths. She understood for the first time in her life that she was somehow on track towards a purpose. It was still too early to put a finger on, but she felt relieved that she was alive and still capable of making a difference.

The only other soul on the shoreline was a bearded man in a robe pushing a cart loaded to the gills with dead bodies. He was tramping in long sweeping passes, searching for other missing family members. Nikki's senses focused on him with the lucidity of a slow motion picture film. Watching him push his lifeless children

98

around in circles brought clarity to the fact that there were thousands of individuals who'd lost their loved ones. The surreal scene, like a photograph from the cover of National Geographic, inspired an idea of how she could help.

She motioned the man over to her, but when he didn't react she rushed to stop him in his path. After unsuccessfully trying to explain herself, she pulled at him until he began to follow her up the hill to the hospital. He began to catch on and grew more excited with each step, wondering which of his two missing sons was waiting for him at the shelter. When he saw the crumbling hospital resting on the skyline like a battle hardened fortress, he ditched his cart on a street corner and grabbed Nikki's hand. Together, they sprinted the final half-mile to the main entrance.

Bursting through the doors, Nikki stumbled into the crowd with one mission in mind, searching the tile floors from corner to corner for her prize. She finally spotted Uzzal sleeping under a registration desk on a disheveled mat. But when she pointed at him in triumph, the old man looked at her with astonishment in his eyes. It was not his son and he frowned at her with cavernous rage. And when he noticed the boy's missing leg, his disappointed boiled over and he slapped Nikki across the face, spat on her feet, and limped out of the hospital. Nikki watched from a shattered window as he returned to the street corner and began pushing the rolling coffin along the rutted road, heading towards nowhere.

Nikki was crushed by her lesson in miscommunication; she'd tried to foster a simple act of kindness and failed. However, a few days later the man would return for the boy after he discovered that his bloodline was no more. His change of heart and subsequent act of humanity may have been what saved Nikki's life.

On that first evening of the aftermath, she had nothing left to do but join the makeshift machines surrounding Nathan's bedside. She was unusually quiet, and by dusk she'd made it clear she preferred to take the nightshift alone. Billy and Charge were more than happy to take a break from their posts, so Nikki spent the humid evening wiping Nathan down with a cool cloth while singing soft melodies in his ear. The hospital grew quiet in the dank air and she rested her head on his chest, allowing her silent sobs to pour over him. And as she dozed off, she swore she saw his eyelids twitch as she repeatedly murmured a pledge of love in his ear.

Vows of love turned to menacing thoughts and fluid dreams. She saw the splendid look in her own eyes the moment she heard Nathan singing below her parent's pasturelands on the night they met. Yet she had rejected him out of fear. Not a fear of happiness, but a concern that she'd met the man she wanted to marry before living a life free from boundaries, before building enough memories on the other side of the reckless edge. How selfish, cruel, ugly she was. How pathetically self-centered. Dark voices pounded in her head with drum-like beats, repeating the truth that it was her fault. Nathan was lying in a coma because she wanted to fuck around with an intriguing guy before settling down. But the only thing breaking free from her boundaries was self-loathing, as untapped tear ducts drained from the veins of her soul.

The dream faded and refocused, and suddenly she was on a magnificent coast, watching Nathan's funeral from out-of-body. As the mourners pointed at her with blame and malice, (many of them dark eyed corpses she'd seen drowned along the streets) she watched as her figure pulled out a bottle of tablets from Billy's stash and then walked into the gaping sea.

The next thing she knew Billy was standing over her, gently shaking her awake. He had been watching her curled on Nathan's chest, and a touch of jealousy flashed through his mind until he reminded himself why he'd come. He stumbled down to her side and whispered, "Nikki, I have to talk to you."

"Huh, what, what is it Billy?"

His words were slurred and his breath stank of Bangla Mad. "Listen, I can't take this shit anymore. The whole scene's bringing me down. So Charge and I are taking off tomorrow, there's a bus headed to Dhaka in the morning. From there, we should be able to fly out of this piss hole. Do you still have your passport or did you lose it in the storm?"

She replied in a soft but harsh tone, "What're you saying? You're willing to leave all these people to die when you have the cash to help them?"

"Listen, this is more than I bargained for, it's not my idea of how I can change the world. Hell, look at these people, most of 'em are dead anyway, what more can I do?"

She looked down at the discolored tubes sticking out of Nathan's mouth and nose, unable to believe Billy was talking like this in front of his mate. She rose to face him eye to eye and asked,

"And what do you suppose we'll do with Nathan you piker, leave him here to die?"

He raised his voice a bit, "Stop this shit, Nikki. I'm not a heartless prick like you're leading on. I've given Dr. Faizabad a lot of money to look after him. He's gonna set him up in a suite when things get back to normal around here. We'll come get him when things get better, as soon as he wakes up."

"And what about his family? Are you going to contact them, at least tell them where their son is?"

"I'll let the authorities take care of that if he doesn't make it. Why worry them when he still has a chance. There's nothing they could do anyway."

"You egotistical creep, there's always something you can do. He's your mate, your bud, and there's no one else like him in this world." Tears were again welling in her eyes as she concluded, "Give me a reason to like you anymore Billy, give me a reason to go with you. Or you can just bugger off!"

The stress and alcohol snapped his easy-going manner. He pointed his finger in her face and growled, "Listen, this was his fucking idea in the first place. I didn't beg him to come out to Timbuktu to surf with Poseidon, so get off my back. I saved his life...we...saved his fucking life last night, does that count for anything?"

"Of course it does, but..." She stopped herself, deciding to test him to see just how low he would go. "Hey, I think we should at least get him the hell out of here and get him to a real hospital before we go."

Billy seemed reassured. "Yah, that's a good idea. I'll make arrangements first thing in the morning."

Nikki poured on her syrupy enthusiasm. "And once that's settled, once we stick him in some hole in Dhaka, we'll carry on with our endless summer vacation to the island of our dreams, like nothing ever happened."

"Right on. I'll take you to Fiji; I know I promised you a stay in one of those bungalows with the glass bottom floors. I'll tell you what, no partying, no games, no drugs. Just the two of us and a bottle of wine."

With scorn dripping from her lips, she said, "Cheers to you, Billyboy, cheers to you." Then her eyes shot him the daggers of a warrior. "You're leaving these people in their time of need! You're leaving your best friend behind. And you expect me to be all bloody romantic. How pathetic." She wanted to slap him across the face, she wanted to shake the earth's axis and change things to how they should be, but all she could do was turn over and curl up on the edge of the bed. She looked at Billy a last time and said, "Go on and get out of here, I'll take care of him myself."

Billy had finally stepped out of his ego long enough to realize just how let down she was. "I'm sorry you feel this way Nikki. But when you change your mind, we'll hook up again and it'll be like old times."

She picked up a glass and threatened to throw it at him, and he finally got the hint. As he exited, he made his final plea. "I'll talk to you tomorrow morning ok? You might have thought things through by then."

But he wasn't a man of his word. The next morning she awoke with a note stuffed in her blouse. It read:

Dear Nikki,

Sorry how things turned out last night. I wish I could care as much as you, but all this death is driving me down. I want you to know that Nathan is like a brother to me. Seeing him like this makes me ill, but I have to heal from this crazy experience in my own way. As for you, you'll always have a place right next to me on our adventures. The truth is, I'm madly in love with you, and need you here on these journeys to feel whole. But I understand what you're going through, so do what you have to do to make yourself feel better. And someday soon, we'll be together again living our dreams.

All my love,
Billyboy

Nikki crumbled up the letter and let out a whimpering cry. Dr. Faizabad peaked in the room, showing his false sense of concern, but she ordered him to leave. She held Nathan's hand, knowing she was utterly alone in a broken land. With no options left, she felt compelled to go back down to the shoreline to try to find the courage to go on.

While looking out over the ocean's surface, Nikki decided to call Nathan's family. She spent the rest of the day searching for an operational phone line. Late that evening, she dialed the number and heard a concerned feminine voice pick up the phone on the other end of the world. Feeling a sudden surge of panic, she lied to Nathan's mom, claiming that he was alright and that he'd asked her to call because he was overwhelmed with helping victims. His mom was suspicious and started asking questions, so Nikki excused herself and got off the phone. But her lies made her all the more determined to nurse Nathan back to health.

For the next several weeks, Nikki continued her ritual of morning walks down to the coast. Some locals had begun to put together cable bridges to get around above the flowing ruins, but she preferred to stroll right through the devastated areas. All around town, new-carving streams continued to make their way back to the polluted sea. As days passed, many of the fleshy landmarks remained fixed in their resting places. At one spot, where a rivulet intersected her trail, there were stacks of rotting cattle that had created a dam and waterfall. Rigor mortise had set in and two of their stiffened legs had met to form an enduring cross. In time, she began to consider this her temple of death, her connection to the lost souls, for she had grown used to the nauseating stench of human and animal flesh. She'd often stare through the water into their bulging eyes, looks of fear fading from glossy pupils, and wonder why death was so final. With no support system to rely on, Nikki was turning to self-imposed idols for answers.

But of all the bodies she came across, there was one in particular that stood out. Each morning, she passed the corpse of a bloated baby rotting in the hot sun at the edge of where the beach had been. Caked with black mud, legs spread wide with indignity, pretty ponytails parting her black hair, her loss of innocence was the epitome of the disaster. So it seemed natural for Nikki to form a bond with the little girl. She even named her new friend, calling her Baby Lynn after a doll she'd had as a little girl. She would stop and talk to the girl every morning, asking questions about spirit and heaven, remaining motionless for hours until she heard the answers she was searching for.

One morning Nikki became openly distraught when she discovered that Baby Lynn was gone, the little girl had become a tiny part of a mass grave dug by bulldozers. While the city attempted to find itself through massive clean up efforts, Nikki's raw emotions became more unhinged each day. There was nothing left to do except face the reality in which she lived. She wandered along the edge of insanity, but her misery drove her to participate in unrivaled relief efforts. After the old man came back for Uzzal, she redoubled her efforts to secure all displaced children into homes. While mingling with the orphans, she began to pick up important elements of the Bengali language. It began with single words. Help: *sahajjo*. Eat: *khawa*. Child: *bachcha*. Live: *jibito*. Soon, she was speaking simple sentences and eventually was carrying on full conversations with the kids about their missing family members.

There was enough work to lose herself for the next thirty years. Over 138,000 people had lost their lives to the typhoon as entire villages were forever wiped from the map. It was impossible for the local governments to form a plan for the millions who were left parentless, penniless, and homeless. Despite her lessons in

106

human suffering and her flirtation with madness, Nikki was growing tough in her resolve and skilled in her ability to give aid. She was learning how to repress her emotion by working herself to exhaustion, becoming robotic in her desire to forget the pain by helping the children. She relished the few success stories along the way, and was especially proud of the time she single handedly reunited a father with his lost daughter. However, most of the time she found herself passing out health kits, relief supplies, and food packets to the refugees. The more days that passed, the less hope there was of reuniting families. Regardless of her task, she was gaining quite a reputation for her ceaseless energy. The local youths began to call her, *Shudor Bir*, or Beautiful Hero. Secretly, she felt more fulfilled than ever before.

Despite working twelve to fifteen hour days, Nikki never allowed her efforts to get in the way of her care for Nathan, and she spent every night by his side. She often sang in his ear until she drifted off to sleep, and although he showed no signs of improvement, she believed he was listening. It was the last flicker of hope that she refused to let die, the only part of her spirit that she allowed to remain soft. Midway through her second month of service, she was prepared herself mentally to carry on with the mechanical mindset for the rest of her life.

And then late one night, everything changed when Nathan suddenly opened his eyes.

## 9

Nikki felt an overpowering sense of relief when she saw the life in Nathan's eyes. Pools of regret, grief, and guilt drained from her conscience, for God had proven his hand in miracles. She wept for sweet joy and mused, "Oh Nathan, I knew you'd wake up. I knew you were still here."

He was weak and foggy, but found his voice. "Nikki, is that you? My God, it's nice to see you." There was a bit of a drawl in his speech and he had lost his self-assurance, but clearly he still had his mind.

She squeezed him for a long time, allowing deep sighs to seep into his warm skin, holding him like a child who's found her lost teddy. After a while, she asked, "Do you know how you got here?"

He paused, casting his thoughts to the lost expanse of time. "Not exactly, but I have a pretty good idea." Then he reeled in his memory. "Last thing I remember, an enormous wave threw me over the falls. I hit the water so hard I must have blacked out. Did you see what happened next?"

"Yah, I thought you met Your Maker, I mean no one could have survived that fall."

"Then how'd I get back in the boat?"

"We tried to find to you, but really it was pure luck. We were stuck in the same giant set and you washed right to us. So Charge went in again after ya."

"He's never gonna let me live that down. Where is he anyway?"

"Well, you've been out for weeks, mate. And you know those blokes, they're off having their kicks back on the ship."

"So why'd you stay here with me?"

She glanced up at the light in the ceiling, releasing the emotion that had been trapped inside for so long. "The storm was maddening enough, but when I saw your pale face, I felt colly wobbles like never before. I knew it wasn't your time, so I started breathing for you."

"So you saved my life?"

"I wouldn't say that, you're just lucky you didn't knacker off in front of me or I would'a kicked you in the tail." Nathan smiled and started to chuckle. Nikki asked, "What's so funny Mr. Bubbly?"

"Well, I never thought our first kiss would be quite like that."

"You didn't think I'd taste your lips for the fun of it, did ya."

"I only hoped, I guess."

Nikki changed the subject. "Nathan, do you remember anything else while you're were down under? I say, do you know what's going on here in this country?"

"Hmmm. It's strange. Mostly I was in Neverland, but there were times when I heard voices, songs of some sort, but I couldn't understand them. It was like they were coming from a different world."

"They probably were, mate. And believe me, you were in a better place than here. I've been alone in my misery for weeks, trying to help all these people that lost their families and homes, but hoping for nothing else in this world but for you to come out of your sleep."

"Thank you Nikki, I knew that somehow. I think that's why I refused to pass on, because believe me, my body and mind wanted to."

Nikki didn't go to the shelters that morning, but spent the day conversing with Nathan about all that she'd seen and done in the past month. She hinted at a feeling of desertion by Billy and Charge, but defended Billy's honor for his financial support. She downplayed the level of care she'd given the children of Chittagong, but Nathan praised her for what she'd accomplished in so short a time. He asked how she was able to hold up through all she'd been through. Given an avenue into her heart's trauma, Nikki began to unleash intimate accounts of praying to decaying cows and talking to dead children.

Nathan was astonished at the depth of her suffering. He used all his strength to reach up and touch her shoulder, promising that as soon as he was able, he'd stretch himself to the limits to help the victims of the typhoon. The rest of the day passed by pleasantly, and by early evening they were nestled side by side in Nathan's tiny bed. Nikki crashed out quickly and slept soundly for the first time in weeks; Nathan however, struggled to find his peaceful place as bewildered thoughts rushed through his mind.

The next morning, Nikki awoke early and whispered that she had to go see her kids. Nathan asked if there was anything he could do there, but she told him to just focus on getting better. He begged her not to go, so she kissed him on the forehead and assured him that she'd be back in the evening to nurse him back to health.

It was a lonely day for the young man, one of the worst of his life. He grew restless and irritable, and tried several times to get out of bed even though he was still too weak to sit up. He had to spend the day staring at the ceiling, imagining what he'd do the next time he was able to catch a wave and wondering if Nikki had finally fallen for him. For a time, he convinced himself that his plan had worked to perfection, but as the steamy day wore on he began to doubt her motivation, fearing that she only felt sorry for him. Growing more and more miserable, he began to see himself as a helpless invalid, just another one of her burdens. He wished he could help her, please her, but more than that, he just wanted to be a part of her life.

Nikki kept her promise, returning early that evening with a plate of rice, dal, and fish as well as a fresh set of stories to tell. Nathan tried to listen to her tales with enthusiasm while hiding his feelings of inadequacy. But he was jumping out of his skin, believing his one chance at happiness was slipping by him. When the next day passed the same as the first, Nathan told himself he would have to do something drastic.

On the third morning, as the dreary pattern began to take hold, Nathan could no longer handle the idea of Nikki leaving him or coming back to him out of guilt. So an hour after she left, he willed himself to his feet and began dragging himself down the hall. Although he could barely walk and his speech was still slurred, his sudden revival was nothing short of phenomenal. Unwilling to miss

111

another moment of life, he set out to find Nikki and become her right hand man.

After some puzzling interactions and more than one dead end, he gained insight to the locale of the renowned *Shudor Bir*. A half hour later, he was lookinng at Nikki through a crude fence as she read a story in Bengali to a group of dark-skinned orphans. Nathan felt a warmth inside more powerful than the emotions elicited from the gut-wrenching documentary films he used to watch in sociology class. Unable to contain himself a moment longer, he hobbled up to the makeshift facility that she'd helped create. Amid friendly introductions to important local leaders, Nathan perceived that Nikki was taken by his level of concern.

So began a new era for Nathan Jansen. And it was clear from the beginning that he fit right in with the troubled bunch, as he formed intimate connections with the wide-eyed kids. For the next four weeks, his endless patience, ceaseless play, and carefree attitude showed the children a spark of hope. But more than anything else, he gave them the gift of laughter. He still hadn't regained his strength or balance so he often found himself tripping over chicken wire or slipping on a loose board, to the delight of every little one around. His naturally athletic body would not function the way he asked it to so he repeatedly mocked himself by sketching flopped sporting performances and failed physical activities. Once, while trying to tell a story with extended hand gestures, he fell backwards off a bench and threw his cane over his head, then sat there and laughed as all the children piled on. Yes, Nathan brought a little joy to a very hard situation as his self-deprecating ways and silly artwork made rough days in the dilapidated shelter more bearable.

Nikki would sometimes watch him from afar, for she saw him as a changed man. It was clear that he was making the most of every moment; after all, he was just happy to be alive, and wanted to share that joy with others who could relate to the wonder of survival. The kids considered him a perfect compliment to their Beautiful Hero, and soon began to call him *Hashshokawr Purush*, or Funny Man.

Nathan and Nikki settled into a busy routine of sheltering, feeding, teaching, and playing with the children. On some days, they'd leave the shelter to make connections with prospective parents or scour the land for displaced victims. Nathan prepared himself to carry on with the demanding pursuits for the rest of his life. Many times, he experienced the most fulfilling moments in his young existence, but also some of the saddest. Too often, he had to face the stress, disappointment, disease, and death that had become a part of everyday life. And the more he tried to talk to Nikki about the situation each evening, the more he understood how thoroughly burnt out she was. Her exhaustion drove him to work double time, rededicating his energy to her responsibilities when she couldn't carry on.

Then one morning, minutes after a favorite toddler named Aniqa died of a fever, Nikki collapsed from emotional fatigue. As Nathan ran to her, he grasped for the first time just how much the strain of daily life had drawn her features and thinned her body. He gathered her in his arms and carried her to the broken down shed behind the schoolhouse that was acting as a medical center. She insisted she was fine and tried to get back to her obsession with saving the children, but he forced her to take a break from her work because it was killing her. When she opened to him, he helped her realize that she needed to heal before she could push herself to further extremes. She was fixated on the fact that there was so much more she could do, yet began to understand that in her current state, she had done enough. Able to relax and breathe for the first time in months, broad ideas of serving the world's children began surface in her imagination.

A few days later, she approached Nathan while he was alone fetching a bucket of water. She looked at him with eyes full of sorrow and asked, "Do you know why I went with you blokes on this crazy trip?"

He stared at her as the bucket swayed back and forth in his hand. "I thought I knew for a while, but I'm not so sure anymore."

"See, it's not what you think. I've tried desperately to get past something that's been eating away at me for too long and it's time I spilled my guts to ya."

"Tell me."

"Well Nathan, I lost my kid sister Kiri a few years ago while she was in my care."

"What do you mean you *lost her*?"

"She died Nathan, fell off a cliff and broke her back. I did everything I could to get down the gorge to reach her, but I couldn't make it. I had to leave her there screaming in pain while I ran for help. But we were five miles in. By the time my rellies came for her, she had already passed. It might as well have been me, because I died too in that moment. And I still blame myself for allowing her out of my reach on that trail."

"But you can't…"

Her eyes were closing, red with tears. "The problem now is that all these little ones suffering, this disease all around me, it brings those emotions back even stronger."

Staring stunned into her open mouth, he tried to say something comforting. "Nikki, I'm sorry."

"Yes, me too."

"But you've done so much to make up for it. Please don't blame yourself anymore."

She whispered back, "But there's no one else to blame. Their innocent looks tell me so every day." Wiping her tears away, she tried to shift the topic to cover her anguish. "So what do you want to do now?"

"I don't understand?"

"Next I mean?"

He attempted to stay with her shifting emotions. "Well, I thought tomorrow we'd try to find that little village to the north you told me about."

She shook her head. "No Nathan. Honest to Christ, I'm ready to take off; I've had as much of death as I can take for a while. I love these kids with all that I am and want to find each of them a home. And I'll be back when I can give them all of myself once again. But I mourn Kiri every time one of my children dies."

"What are you saying?"

"I don't know what I'm saying. I guess I need a holiday in order to recharge. How about we run off together for a spell?"

"Where do we go?"

"I bet Fiji would be beautiful this time of year."

Although he loved what he was doing and felt like he was finally giving back to the world, his deepest wish was sitting there selfishly for him to grab. He thought about asking her to return to New Zealand where the two of them could take a break from the world at her parent's ranch. But he didn't want her to change her mind, so he asked, "How would we get to Fiji?"

Nikki didn't hesitate. "Why, with Billy's help, of course."

Nathan hoped it would just be the two of them on their island getaway, but he didn't have the nerve to ask about her relationship with Billy. He wanted her to break free from Billy's anchor, at least until she was emotionally stable enough to handle his unpredictable antics. Of course, he had to admit he was pretty excited by the thought of getting back to the island ways. He missed the pleasures of the open ocean and believed he was healthy enough to surf again. They talked it through later that night, and he gave her the word to get a hold of their connection to the better life.

After two weeks of subtle hints, endless guilt, and counting down to the departure date, Nikki gathered everyone around the meeting rug. She made a short speech describing the immeasurable impact the children had had on her. She then handed a volunteer a hefty cash donation, and explained that with the gracious contribution from Billy Windsor, they could break ground on a permanent site for an orphanage. There were cheers and shouts of joy, but also a lot of tears when she revealed it would be her last day with them.

Throughout the small feast and honor ceremony, the mood was somber. Nathan tried to lighten the air by taking candid pictures of Nikki with each child and goofy shots of himself. He led them in singing songs and talking about joyful times. Nikki capped off the evening by presenting a large box of toys and stuffed animals to the children that she'd received from an overseas relief crate. By nightfall, she knew it was time to go. Despite her inner sense of relief, she had a terrible time saying goodbye to the kids, holding them in her arms well into the evening. Nathan took her hand and promised they'd return someday soon; the children watched with blurry eyes as the two of them disappeared into the darkness.

Nathan had one thing left to do before leaving Bangladesh. Early the next morning, he borrowed a small boat from a local fisherman and took it out to where he had nearly lost his life. There, he meditated on all he had seen and done in his short life, and thanked God for the opportunities he'd been given, especially Nikki. He sat there in the still water just before sunrise and allowed the hopeless feeling of going over those massive falls to come rushing back. With generations of fear passing through him, he promised himself that he would again appreciate his life.

That day, after a jarring bus ride along potted roads, the couple found themselves in the Dhaka Airport where two first class tickets to Bali were waiting for them.

Nathan was surprised and asked, "I thought you said we were going to Fiji?"

Nikki hid her disappointment. "It seems Billy and the crew just left there last week." She knew full well Billy had gone there without her out of spite, but she forged a sense of excitement. "So we're going to meet up with them in Bali and take a coastal tour of the islands of Indonesia. You know, Timor, Java, Sumatra. A bit more precarious, but a beautiful area nonetheless. Great waves too."

He sensed the quiver in her voice and asked, "Are you sure you're ready to go Nikki?"

She paused on the tarmac, overlooking the steamy country lying before her like a menacing mirage, and said, "I am, Nathan. I am." But after taking a few steps up the stairs she turned to the daunting jungle and whispered, "Beautiful children of Bangladesh, I hope you know I did my best for you."


10.


Indonesia, a land of rapid wilds and raw faith. One look at the ancient shrines and mosques peaking out like multi-layered sandcastles from the rich soil, and you'll realize that somewhere along the way human conviction grew entwined with the landscape. As you become immersed in the diverse and primitive cultures, you may begin to recognize how stringent dogma lost out to simple existence within the spirited jungles. And if you have ever questioned your god or the gods of mankind, you may see just how creation can be trumped by survival. Yes, if you dig deep enough, you may witness how Jesus met Buddha. How Buddha met Rama. And as the holy trinity, the enlightened one, and the reincarnated idol occupy the land in a simultaneous and evolving state of coexistence, you may begin to understand their wonderful myths in action.

Nathan looked out the window in a state of awe as the single engine aircraft flew just above sun-shading treetops and triangular temples. On the ground, densely forested centers of worship were teeming with elusive creatures, like disconnected kingdoms attempting to cooperate on a far off planet. Home to sherbet-tinged birds, alien-like insects, extinct miniature tigers, and the last of the real dragons, the exquisite chain of islands truly believes in nothing more than animalism herself, although she holds an ancient mystique concerning God that can not be described, but must be experienced to accept as truth. All these images flashed through Nathan's mind, stirring his imagination with an overabundance of natural and cultural wisdom that would one day develop into song. Finally, he understood how much his priorities had changed since leaving the comfort zone of his former life. The plane passed over island after incredible island and then set down on a narrow runway on the outskirts of Bali, and he felt as if he had once lived there long ago.

It was a short five mile walk from the airport to the agreed upon meeting place on the southern tip of the island. Nathan and Nikki took in the flourishing sites and verdant aromas from the ground, and were elated to be back in the raptures of nature despite the dense population. Nikki's fresh sense of wonder and adventure allowed Nathan to open unreservedly to his fun-loving and witty self.

At some point they wandered off the beaten path, playing in the rainforest, exploring a series of caves, and splashing around in the crystal blue tide, lost in the moment as if they were on a private rendezvous. The highlight of the day came when they ascended the oceanfront cliffs of Uluwatu and stumbled upon a group of mischievous monkeys. The primordial rush was as startling as it was entertaining as they watched the primates swinging, flirting, skirting, and flinging three hundred feet above the coast without a care in the world. But the occasion came to an abrupt halt when Nathan went around for a closer look and found himself gaping at the face of a startled adolescent. The combination of the little bugger's shrieks of warning and Nikki's shrieks of laughter quickly scared the other monkeys off into the higher trees.

By early evening, the couple was talking over a bottle of wine while Nathan's fingers stroked Nikki's knee and their feet dangled high above the sea. Gradually, their conversation shifted to more personal matters and Nikki let her long-standing fear of intimacy slip out between sighs. It was such a perfect setting that she began to feel the urge to lean in and kiss him. But as the sun throbbed on the point of their field of vision, drawing them in with its celestial magnetism, Charge's Zodiac appeared in the distance. The boat skated towards them like a black water bug, and Nathan knew the moment was over, although he'd never lived a finer day.

Charge kept the throttle buried until he ran upon the beach at full speed. He jumped out of the craft before it came to a complete stop and wrapped his tree trunk arms around each of them with a powerful bear hug. He was grateful to see them; the tough-guy exterior melted away as his gnawing sense of guilt and responsibility were finally pacified by the presence of true friends. His features lightened with childlike excitement when he asked Nathan what it was like to cheat death. Nathan avoided the question, choosing to thank him for pulling him out of the ocean a third time. Had he looked more closely, he might have noticed a thin trail from a tear on Charge's cheeks.

While they made their way out to the infamous *Rumrunner*, Charge mumbled something about, "Getting back to the way things used to be." They couldn't have understood what he meant at the time, but they were excited to give their old lives a go.

The ship was anchored in a secluded bay surrounded by China-hat hills and coral-white beaches. Low-lying clouds streaked with pink and violet filled their vision as they approached the magnificent vessel. When they climbed aboard, Nathan thought it odd that no one was around to greet them, although he was thankful it was so quiet. Charge snickered and said that maybe Billy escorted the gang to shore so the twosome could have time to rest. Nathan was thrilled. How fantastic it would be to spend a secluded evening with Nikki, soaking up the ship's luxuries without the obligation to socialize.

But when Charge asked them to grab a few drinks at the bar below deck, they made their way down to the end of the dark stairwell, opened the game room door, and their quiet night exploded in front of them. Just as a deafening "Surprise!" shook them in their tracks, several men wearing masks, wild island garb, and brandishing spears jumped out from the darkness. Silvery confetti fluttered by his periphery while deep fears of snarled fangs, protruding noses, and spiked teeth dropped Nathan to his knees.

or six torchbearers appeared from the shadows, standing erect over Nathan as Nikki tried to help him off the floor.

There were shouts and cheers and laughter, but Nathan's mind had yet to sort the chaos. His vision was filled with images of shield-like heads, oblong faces, and bugged-out features. Some masks were moving towards him, and dozens more were floating in midair or hanging from hooks on walls. He turned away from the phantoms, but when he glanced up towards the ceiling, he saw two or three creatures gawking back at him from the deep-set skylight. One by one, they dropped to the ground, and as the partygoers began to dance around him while lingering chants of "Resurrection" rang in his ears, he stood frozen in disbelief.

There were over fifty people rushing at him, more than double than had been on the ship at any other time. Although their faces were covered with traditional costume, it was clear there were many new bodies under Billy's command. Most of them wore tight bikinis, slinky dresses, and steamy tribal paint complimenting their sensual masks. Yes, Billy had been a busy man indeed.

Nathan was struggling to cope with his sudden center stage status, but Nikki was amused with the morbid theme of the party. She smiled at his bumbling ways and kissed his cheek to try to wipe the terror from his eyes. The crowd parted as Billy leaped and twirled in colorful motion; then approached his guests of honor like a lurking animal. He was fully engrossed in his altered state of role-play, wearing the mask of the shaggy lion-dragon Barong and holding the mask of the female witchdoctor Rangda. The two god-like characters were longtime favorites of Balinese dancing tradition.

As the drumbeats faded and grew silent, he stood in front of Nathan, took off his alter ego, and put his arms around his friend. He looked deep into Nathan's eyes and said, "Welcome back my brother, I missed you."

Nathan was finally able to catch his breath. He replied, "I missed you too my friend."

The tender moment exposed a rare passage of suffering holed up in Billy's heart. He continued, "I thought you were gone man, I really thought I lost you. And I couldn't have handled that right now."

Nathan was flattered by Billy's sincerity but embarrassed by all the attention, so he tried to lighten the mood. "Thanks for the party bud, but can I ask what's up with the freaky masks?"

Billy's eyes widened and he let that shit-eating grin of his flare in the flaming light. "Hey man, it's a dead man's party!"

"Oh yah?"

"That's right. This was all my idea, you like it?"

"Yah Billy thanks…I guess."

"Don't you see, this is all for you, you came back from the dead so we're throwing you a bash from the other side, Bali style."

"You didn't have to do all this man, just letting me back on your boat is enough for me."

But Billy wouldn't let lie the fragile state of his guilt. "Your always welcome here. And I'll tell you this, I'll be there for you until the day I die."

After slamming a third shot, Charge chimed in, "Yah, it's like you're our Jesus, having you come back now is like a celebration with your ghost."

They could find any reason to party. Nathan felt a twinge of discontent, wondering if he had outgrown the whole scene. He was beginning to understand that sometimes when things return to the way they used to be, they can never be the same again. But all he could say was, "Believe me, I'm not Jesus."

After his heartfelt release, Billy's simmering emotions were quieted back to their charming source. He motioned to an attractive young lady in white waiting in the shadows a few feet off. He winked at Nathan and said, "Good, because everything you see in front of you is yours. Now relax, give in, and let us take you where you've already been, past the edge of heaven and to the world of bliss. Prepare yourself, I grant you the gift of ecstasy, pleasure, and physical freedom."

With that, six of the largest men in the ballroom clutched Nathan by the limbs while four women ripped off his Aloha shirt and tied him down on a cushioned platform with silky ribbons. Charge poured thin streams of a clear, icy liquor over his head and into his mouth while others blew blasts of potent smoke into his nose and lungs.

So began Billy's ceremony for the only man he truly admired other than his grandfather. Nathan noticed Nikki smiling at his side so he went along for the ride without a trace of resistance. In fact, he closed his eyes, took in a few deep breaths and allowed himself to enjoy the massaging motions of masculine hands and tickling sensations of feminine fingers.

With Nathan at ease, Billy held up his arms to quiet the crowd. The torchbearers centered their flames in a band of fire above his head, and Billy placed the mask of the benevolent warrior Barong over Nathan's face. He treated the act as if it were a rite of passage, a transformation from life to death and back again. Nathan might have realized for the first time just how wasted Billy was when his friend began to speak like a medicine man, carrying on about his trip to the other world. He held Nathan's head in his hands and said, "This extraordinary being represents all that is good in the universe, and I call his energy forth to meet in Nathan's soul. Yes, I invite you Barong to live within the boy's body, in order to give him free rein, eternal peace, and everlasting happiness."

The crowd began to chant as Billy brought forward the female figure wearing nothing but a ghostly white mask and a creamy string bikini. Billy placed the mask of Rangda over her colorless countenance and laid her hand on Nathan's. Trying to initiate a sacred union, he said, "Powerful and gentle Barong, I offer thee the beautiful witch of revelry and unrest to have your way with." Decadent music began to beat in Nathan's ears as the girl grabbed him by the waist and began to dance around his midsection with grace and ferocity. The power of the smoke and liquor had blurred his judgment to such a degree that thoughts of a romantic evening with Nikki temporarily escaped his mind. His starry-eyed disguise was smiling from ear to ear as the sinful goddess untied his wrists and ankles and led him through the crowd towards her cabin.

But just before the door closed behind him, he saw Billy leading Nikki and the other revelers to the main deck to begin the rest of the festivities. It was in that instant that Nathan realized the girl in white was nothing more than an offering, his low-balled piece of barter for the rights to Nikki. Despite Billy's good intentions, there was always a low-lying ulterior motive for his actions. Whether he aware of it or not, he just couldn't carry out an unconditional act of kindness without a personal hook.

Nathan's mysterious friend took off her mask and pulled on the string in back of her bikini, showing him a hint of her dark complexion, alluring sensuality, and gentle curves. Her sloping brown eyes held him in her grasp as she approached on her knees. She backed him to the corner of the bed, started in on his bare chest, and tried to kiss her way down on him. But all he could think of was Nikki sitting alone with Billy on the main deck. Suddenly, he found his courage to stop the woman mid-flight. She gave him a playful look until he pushed her away a third time.

"What's the matter, am I not hot enough for you?"

"It's not that hon, you're as pretty as they come, but I can't do this. It may sound dumb, but I'm in love with someone else."

She looked at him oddly and asked, "Luv? Does that matter on this boat? You come over here and I teach you about love."

Despite the excitement rushing into his loins, he got up and headed towards the door. She was offended by his rejection and launched a mini bottle of vodka at the wall behind him. Before closing the door, he turned, threw a towel back her way and said, "I don't know what matters on this ship anymore, but I sure the fuck hope something does."

The contrast between this life and the life he had been entrenched in only days ago was shocking. As he crept up the stairs, he promised himself he'd never again compromise the value he placed on Nikki's companionship. He knew once and for all that another beautiful body would simply never appease him. More than anything else in the world, he needed to separate Billy from Nikki.

But when he got to the rim of the outlining crowds celebrating around their smiling faces at the open bar, he lost his nerve. Seeing Nikki messing with Billy caused that panicked feeling of betrayal to invade his chest once more. He had no other choice but to sneak away to watch the action from the crow's nest. No one noticed him climb the rope ladder in the darkness, and soon he was hiding in his secret perch above the ocean. Brilliant fireworks exploded above his head and hot ashes began falling in his hair each time the wind shifted direction. The war of emotions began to erupt inside his insecure world. He looked down upon the laughter and festivities and understood that Billy was giving Nikki a welcoming party of epic proportion. How could he ever compete with such a lifestyle?

Nathan spied on their every move like a madman, taking mental snapshots of their flirting and frolicking, dancing and doting, until he almost vomited from what he saw. Dark thoughts began to seep into his mind; their interaction reminded him of the outlandish monkeys from earlier that day. Yes, she would always end up at Billy's side, because he had the money, the grace, and the gift of gab. So why did he come back to put himself through such torture? Why was he letting her slip through his fingers yet again?

Unable to bear it any longer, Nathan turned to watch the circus of colorful personalities as they played together like a sociology project gone wild. Collectively, the crowds were lost in their frames of fantasy and bright costume, exotica and blurred reality. Soon, he realized that they were not all play-acting, as a group of natives from the surrounding islands reminded him of the Tahitian stowaways from *Mutiny on the Bounty*. He tracked the four chiseled men looking to make trouble and stir up the ambiance. After striking out with a couple of blondes, they began to mingle with the hired Bali dancers performing along the outside deck.

Amid animalistic catcalls and aggressive come-ons, the hub of the party shifted around their action like a buzzing current of human energy. With quivering hip shakes and crude belly jiggles, they joined the stylistic dancers, mocking their talents. All eyes grew fixed on a particularly gifted showgirl, her flowering headdress, ornate outfit, and sleek gyrations sending chills down men's spines. Despite the interruptions, she showed up the bad boys, deflecting their negative attention with her easy grace and flow. The rabble joined her in her snaking moves, crowding on top of the bar and balancing on tables until one collapsed under the heavy pressure. Nathan had to snigger for it was clear that the party had reached its critical mass.

With the crowds in full swing, it was Charge's turn to take the stage. He led a group of five drunkards up and out over the arches accenting the whirlpools and waterfalls. Nathan was surprised that none of them saw him as they hung at nearly eye level with him at the stern of the ship. They held on for eons, but one by one dropped into the pool, pulling off ugly dives and spattering cannon balls amid excited roars from the crowd.

Despite the sideshows, Nathan's internal warning system kept bringing him back to the middle ring. Whenever his mind forced his eyes upon her, there she was, tormenting him like a magnificent addiction. Nikki had gotten sucked in by the wave of action and had fallen right back into the old scene. He asked himself over and over why he'd agreed to go back to the fucking ship. He saw things differently now; he was beginning to grow up. Everyone was beautiful in Billy's life, but no one was really beautiful at all. Their lifestyle was a self-fulfilling ride into reckless abandon, an overwhelming and all encompassing venture into the darkest freedoms. Extended time with Billy was a one-way journey through bliss, an adventure that would take your life away while you were living it.

The merciless torture came to a climax when Nikki grabbed Billy's hand and led him off into the night air to be alone. Nathan decided he'd seen enough, and told himself that he'd never give himself so fully to anyone again. He caught some flak from a drunk who noticed him making his way down the ladder, and felt the impulse to kick the guy's ass, take his writhing aggression out on the drunk fool. He needed a way out. By the time he reached the deck, the tension made his hands clench in tight agony, and he thought about what it would be like to jump off the ship again. This time, he knew, no one would be there to save him.

But there was a bit more to live for now, at a minimum the knowing that he'd recently escaped death. So instead of going over the rail, he went to seek the support of Kerby, the only man he knew who'd been through more shit than him. While climbing up to the bridge, he accidentally stumbled upon his mentor smoking a bowl. Kerby smirked with starry eyes and a bit of his grizzled beard lit up from a spark. In a startled tone, he whispered, "Why, you're enough to scare the hell right out of me. Do you know what Billy'd do if he saw me here like this?"

"I'm sorry, I just needed to talk to someone."

"Well shit, your first night back and already she's given you the black water blues?"

"It looks that way."

His glossy eyes were bulging. "And you came to *me* to help you figure it all out? What's wrong with you boy?"

"Hey, there's not a lot of choices out here." He laughed out loud and continued, "I mean, I guess Garo'd help me write a song about her or something, but I could use a little more advice than that. Sorry I bothered you though."

"No, no, I'm glad you came my way." Kerby took another long toke of his bamboo pipe and passed it to Nathan. "Do you know what this all means?"

Nathan declined the offering and replied, "No tell me, what's it mean?"

His mentor turned to the sky and blew his smoke into the black heavens. "Man, will you look at those stars! So many of them, imagine what the fuck's going on out there in all those other places."

"Yah, they're great, but what's it all mean?"

"I guess it means you really dig her, that's what. And that's something I don't often find out here in the Seven Seas. That's something you only find in those stars."

"So what do I do about it?"

"If I were you, I'd get the good fuck off this boat before this life destroys you."

"And what about Nikki?"

"Try to get her to come along too, I guess. But I don't think she wants out. She cozies up nicely to this lifestyle. Either way, you're best away from here. You got too much to offer this world. And believe me, this is hard shit for me to say, 'cause I dig having your crazy ass on board."

"Thanks Kerby, that means a lot coming from you."

"Well, I might give good advice, but I don't always follow it for myself. So hey, don't tell anybody about this little powwow, huh? I want to keep my day job."

Nathan reached out a hand to the weathered guru. "Sure man, no problem."

Slipping away from the bridge towards his room, he thought of the underground chaos carrying on in everyone's lives. For Nathan, it was the beginning of a time for coming to terms with many secrets, old and new.

He lay in his bed, pondering Kerby's advice. He knew Nikki would never change; in fact, nothing would ever change. For the first time since leaving home, he admitted to himself that it was his fault. Yes, karma had come knocking on his door and would never forgive him for what he'd done to her. He wondered how she was getting on with life and whether she'd take him back.

It was the closest thing to an arranged marriage one could have in modern day America. It had started harmlessly enough with a blind date; he grew interested because she had a silver spoon up her ass and he found out too quickly that she was good in bed. But as the courtship took off, he began to resent her as nothing more than an extension of his stepfather. She was the daughter of Dale's boss, and Nathan was pressured to rush into a serious relationship. When Nathan found out the prick received a full promotion for his services, he wanted to call off the engagement.

He was heading home to Fresno from Santa Cruz for the wedding rehearsal when his conscience told him enough was enough. Upon leaving campus, he stayed on the Coast Highway rather than veering onto the North 17. Twenty miles later, he stopped at an overlook to make peace with the Pacific Ocean one more time. While staring at the horizon, he felt himself turn the thin band of his engagement ring around and around on his finger.

He thought about all he was and all he secretly wanted to be. It was true a part of his frustration was that he simply wasn't ready to grow up. Like so many young adults, he didn't want to settle for the norm and wanted to live his passions. But it was more than his parent's unreasonable expectations or his general contempt for

Tamara. It was the caged system called human life. Mankind's mindlessness--Authority's rule-- Civilization's engine. The most intolerable part of life was the feelings of worthlessness he kept hidden in his own thoughts. Far-reaching ideas continuously filled his mind, designs for a make-believe society of harmony. But something had always held him back. The intertwining controls kept him from being the person he wanted to be and that made him care little about his future. He wanted to make change but didn't believe people cared enough to take the next step. Yet he hoped his music could make a difference by filling the void.

Without another thought, he took his engagement ring off and tossed it into the seamless blue. For a fleeting second he was compelled to dive in after the shiny symbol before it was lost forever. But the thought of growing old with a mediocre, loveless life pervaded his mind and he didn't move. The wistful center of his soul told him the engagement was off. In fact, his whole life was off. The decision was simple, effortless. No phone calls, no goodbyes, a short letter to Tamara poured through his pen. By the next morning, he was gone for good.

He had to admit, it had been a hell of a ride. Yet, he decided right then that it would be his last night on Billy's ship. Of course he'd wonder what could have been with Nikki for the rest of his life. That tiny spark of optimism pressed so far down in his being wanted to hold onto hope. But in the morning, he'd ask for a ticket back to California so he could try to patch things up with his manic fiancé.

Eventually, he melted away into a sound, unsettled sleep. At the darkest hour, the bustling sensuality left over from his island mistress returned to his dreams. Her specter of sexual energy approached, bound in nothing but her revealing white bikini. But when she climbed on top of him, Nathan discovered she was wearing a mask mimicking Nikki's features. The confusion turned to erotic bliss, and the girl began to touch him in ways that made him quiver. She would take him to the verge, letting him build, swell, until he was an instant from releasing his desire. Then she would pause, going down to kiss his chest and caress his nipples through her mask. Slowly, rhythmically, she began riding him with perfect force and penetration. The dream grew more and more vivid, until he could no longer bear the continuous pleasures.

The truth of his trance-like ecstasy was seeping into his senses. From another world, he felt her long hair tickling his shoulders; he heard two voices moaning as one. There was a gentle stirring and his fantasy began to dissolve back into his tiny sleeping quarters. Opening to semi-consciousness, Nathan discovered that his dream was not a dream. It was Nikki. She was on top of him, making love to him at the most soulful level. While riding him, she reached down to pick up his hands, allowing his fingers to caress her circular breasts. When he saw her elegant features tensing in the shadow of the darkness, he began to kiss every inch of her skin.

It was the first time he truly made love to a woman, discovering pleasure centers that were born from the emotional tides of evolution. There would be no more false fronts, hidden feelings, or unforgivable letdowns. She gave herself to him at all levels, releasing years of apprehension and insecurities. Finally, he understood the secret, powerful affection of a woman.

As she became a part of him, handing him the key to the other half of the human condition, that deeply gentle force of femininity, he understood what it meant to be a man, an element of nature, a ray of God. He pulled her towards his arched upper body until her soft chest was cradling his stubbled face. They climaxed with the force of a tiny eruption, convulsing and flittering in the eternal world of the fairylands. Together, they shared tears of forgotten laughter, throbbing joy, triumphant pain, letting each other dissolve in their magnificent bond.

And as she lay in his arms, vulnerable, fragile, raw, he believed they would share their lives together. When she leaned over and whispered her love in his ear, her feeling of total adoration from the moment they met, he wanted to do nothing more than provide her the 'life eternal' that he saw in her eyes.

Years afterwards, when he realized just how far he let himself fall, he would long for another chance at their precious connection.

11.

The couple stretched awake in the fresh breezes of dawn, blanketed in nothing more than each other's warm skin. While the dreamtime fog cleared, Nathan's excited energy returned, engulfing his masculine mind. He found himself persistently rubbing against Nikki's backside, initiating a morning session of love. She rolled under him, temporarily halting his progress, and snickered, "You randy little devil, have you ever heard of foreplay?"

He rose above her and said, "As far as I'm concerned, *last night* was our foreplay."

She was done playing hard to get, as the untold comfort of his firm body had her in its grip. She tossed her head back and said, "Well, at least put a frenchie on, I'm not quite ready to have a sprog up the duff."

He laughed at her candor, again falling in love with the way her Kiwi accent so perfectly illustrated her persona. And when she let him in, he felt the childlike assuredness of knowing it wasn't all a dream. As the morning sun peaked through their porthole, they silently expressed their deepest physical desires as passionately as they had the first time.

When they were spent, Nathan lay by her side stroking her hair. Eventually, she asked, "So what do we do now?"

He was intrigued by the situation, as his darker half saw the relationship as a way to get back at his self-centered buddy. He shot her a devious stare and said, "We do nothing. Act like nothing's going on between us until we find each other late each night."

"What about Billy?"

"He looks pretty out of it if you ask me. You play your game when he's around and I'll do my thing to keep him in the dark. If he found out what we were up to, he wouldn't let us stay on board another night."

"But why do you want to stay?"

His excitement boiled over. "Because we both know this is a once in a lifetime opportunity. We're seeing the whole world together and can play with each other on a new stage every day. We can have the best of both worlds, until it's time to move on."

Nikki was fascinated and a bit shocked by his proposal. "Luv, you're two sammies short of a picnic. How are we supposed to get away with this?"

"It'll just be for a little while." He paused and pulled her closer. "Listen. Since the moment I met you, it's been my dream to share the magic of the South Pacific with you. Nikki, after all we've been through, we need this."

"All righty, Luv. I'll be happy as long as we're together."

"Don't worry, we'll know when it's time to move on."

"God's truth, it won't be long. But you're right, it's best we make this a day."


Soon after, Nathan aligned himself with Billy, waking him early to get in the water for the first time in months. After a brief search in the Zodiac, they came upon pristine conditions at Dreamland, Bali's most powerful surf spot. And on three consecutive breakout days, it was like old times, as the gang ripped it up on crystal clear tubes.

But when the waves died down and the initial excitement of having Nathan back in his life wore off, Billy was less enthusiastic about being a part of the action. Priorities on the ship had certainly shifted. In fact, Billy was rarely seen during the day, as he slept until evening and stayed up half the night.

So began their underground affair. Perfect Bali mornings unfolded in front of them like liquid fantasy. The secret was certainly easier to keep than Nathan had imagined. Around every mischievous corner they sought the private pleasures of undisclosed passion. Easy hours in the sun were spent anxiously anticipating sleepless nights. And after every lost evening, they'd find their way to each other, lighting the flames of forbidden darkness. When the nighttime festivities made it too risky to meet up, they'd get together in the early morning, sneaking a shower together or slipping under the outdoor bar before dawn.

But it was about more than sexual gratification; it was a time of total fulfillment and complete happiness. Nikki and Nathan grew lost in their private worlds, finding inspiration in the unfolding beauty of every instant, big and small. The blue planet seemed to slow down and open to them, releasing its intention, bringing them to source. This fundamental attraction woke them to the affinity of creation, and within the surreal setting they were able to express their energy through original thoughts and unlimited actions.

As the *Rumrunner* made her way languidly around the tip of Timor and into the Java Sea, reaching the coasts of Alor, Flores, Sumbawa, Java, and eventually Sumatra, there was ample time for contemplation and thrills. Nathan and Nikki found their place somewhere between towing the line and living over the edge. For days, they'd lay in the sun pouring over thought provoking books, tinkering with new melodies, or writing voraciously in a shared journal. When their creative juices were spent, they'd take off for the day to explore uninhabited veins in the heart of the islands. These journeys were raw and unplanned, pumping their blood with wild adventure, taking them as close to the shadowy organ as the

138

modern world would allow. While kayaking down surging rapids, trekking in deep jungles, or swimming under tumbling falls they learned as much about their darker selves as they would have had they been on the Congo at the turn of the Century.

Eventually, the quest for self-discovery and the call for adventure blended into an unquenchable yearning for unrefined and vigorous truth. Although Nathan continued to feel the need to challenge himself at a fundamental level, he no longer did so with a reckless death wish, but with a firm determination for life. Nikki, on the other hand, found her peace of mind within their tireless escapades. While discovering the abounding sights and sounds deep in the corners of a raw paradise, she began to heal from months of tireless trauma.

The turning point came on an early morning boat ride the day before they left Bali when they came across the sun-shrouded silhouette of the Tanah Lot Temple. This elegant structure, built on a section of sea cliff that had long ago broken away from its base, appeared as a holy island when water filled around its perimeter at high tide. Upon arrival, Nathan and Nikki secured the Zodiac on the southern tip of the bastion and climbed the rock staircase through lush scrub bush and budding pink flowers. Then, in the isolated morning air, they sat under a thatched temple that seemed to be growing from the layers of pancake rock like a divine mushroom. While gazing out to the sacred blue, their liberated states of mind merged with the perceptive silence to allow in the insight of ancient gods.

It was then that Nikki revealed her wandering, expanding horizons. She scooted in closer to Nathan and said, "I'm not one to carp, but have you ever felt like a part of you was missing?"

Nathan understood the nature of longing. He answered, "Nikki, since the moment we met, *everything* good was missing from my life. And for too long it was just sitting right there, too close for me to grab a hold of. But now, because of you, I have everything I ever wanted."

"Cheers to you mate, but now that we have each other's company, aren't you ready to take the next step?" She looked to the sky and watched a lone seabird wing by. Nathan thought for a moment she was talking about marriage and kids, but as she went on he understood she was hinting at something quite different. "Don't get me wrong, I'd love to fossick around with you from here to the ends of the earth, but I'd give all this up to do what it is I was put on this planet to do."

"What's that Nikki?"

"Not really certain, Luv. But I felt most alive when I was helping those kids in Chittagong."

"Do you wanna go back there?"

"No, it's not that, it's more that I wish all the children didn't have to suffer in this world. I wish I could start a movement to save every last one of 'em, take them away in a ship like ours and show them the beauty of the sea day after day after day. Keep sailing away until a time when the human race finds what it's missing."

"You already did that for them. I saw the way those kids looked up to you, you were their hero, their savior. You gave them

140

the power to imagine, to hope. Be proud because not many could have done as much."

"That's just it, I feel the bloody need to keep going. Not out of guilt, but out of this new conviction that keeps swirling through my noggin. This temple, these islands, these ancient religions, I can hear them calling to me to give back. I've had a good life and need to share myself with them."

"Then go for it. I only hope I can keep up with all you offer this world because everything in you makes those around you shine."

"You're too much. Helping others just makes me feel alive. I'd love to get to the point when I'm done putting in a tough day's work, I can go out and enjoy myself for me. Put away the gloominess and do things for me. You know, surf, dance, sing, or party without feeling bad about myself. How do I do that?"

"Believe me, I struggle with the same thing if I think too much. I mean I'm not exactly doing a lot with my life right now other than having fun and making great memories."

"Nathan my Luv, what would you do if you could have anything you wanted? I mean, what will you do when you leave our motley crew?"

"I don't know. Haven't thought about it since I left my family and the dreams they forced on me in college." He paused. Nikki gave him an unsatisfied, reproachful look so he smirked, took a deep breath, and prepared to reveal his private dream. "Ok, I'll tell you."

"You will, will ya?"

"See, I'd really love to keep making music. In fact, the reason I went to Hawaii in the first place was to try to find my sound. Then all this excitement and adventure fell into my lap so my music has kind of taken a back seat. But it's all good. Anyway, I know how impossible it is to make it in the industry. So I'm happy doing my little thing on the side and keeping it between friends."

She reached up with a finger and stroked his lips. "Listen mate, if you're serious about it, this voice of yours can do wonders for the world. I'm not pulling your leg, when you sing to me my insecurities melt away like a schoolgirl and I believe I can do anything. You're scary good. From the first, I was afraid of falling in love with you because your words were too velvety, your melodies too perfect. That's why I ran to the closest thing that wasn't like you, I didn't want to get hurt."

Her comments fit the final pieces in place for him, as a sudden excitement jolted him through the heavens. "You know, after listening to what you're saying, I think I feel the same, only in my own way. I want to make a difference as much as you."

"Well silly, maybe your music can do that for people. I don't think you know how talented you really are."

A splendid glow began to resonate along the outline of his features as he looked to the sky and mused, "That would be unbelievable, getting through to people with my music." Then a sudden rush of insecurity broke the rhythm and he mumbled, "But I just wouldn't even know how to begin."

Nikki stopped him in his tracks. "I think you do, but you're just too afraid of the truth."

"What do you mean?"

"I mean Billy. Billy's your ticket to success. He's got the financial backing and he really admires your talent."

"You think so?"

She smiled, "Why else would he put up with your crazy ass if he didn't see the gift in your music?"

"Everyone he hangs with is nuts. I just figured I fit right in."

"Well, you're their late night entertainment in more ways than one. You just keep recording your stuff because it's simply remarkable. And in time, I'll work on Billy."

"What about you, what will you do if I try to pursue a music career?"

"Why, I'll sing with you of course."

"Oh yah?"

"And when we make it big, we'll sing about peace and truth and give free concerts to the children." She kissed him on the lips. "That's right, we'll make a difference together."

Their moment of intimacy was broken when the first straggling tourists waded through knee high water and up to the base of the temple. But as Nathan jokingly thanked the gods for granting them a glimpse of their future, he believed their dreams had been set in motion. He gave Nikki a long hug and asked if she wanted to go for a surf at the base of the sacred fortification. But their conversation compelled her to go ashore to check out the state of the local living conditions.

So while rising musical fantasies stretched Nathan's imagination around the clean little waves, Nikki searched for a way to help an impoverished little girl smile, or a mother secure a meal for her little boy. The songs in Nathan's thoughts were filled with the clear idea that Nikki was allowing herself to become the wonderful human being that she always longed to be. He understood that she was growing into her purpose and nothing could have made him happier. However, he also understood that before long, he'd have to give up the easy life and take the next step towards living *his* dreams.

12.

Despite unlimited avenues into meditation and contemplation, downtime on the ship became more and more agonizing for the lovers. While apart, they secretly pondered the excitement of their last conversation or the possibilities of their next interaction. And because they had to be diligent in their perception, they began to see things in a whole new light, maybe a bit closer to the way they really were. The contrast between their emerging lifestyles and Billy's deepening rut became disturbingly clear. Yet, no one else seemed to mind that he virtually ignored his friends while allowing an influx of groupies on board at every major port for the never-ending party.

More than just the atmosphere on the ship had changed, as the spark of optimism that defined Billy's personality was also gone. His tidy living quarters had become filthy and crowded, no longer with wanna-be surfers but with junkies and moochers. The worst characters huddled together below deck like a swarm of stinking flies, and Billy relentlessly tried to impress them with everything he pretended to be.

Sometimes Nikki had to keep up her appearance as Billy's girl, and couldn't hide her disappointment in how bizarre things had become. She was maturing into a woman, growing tired of their antics, but most importantly, she was clean. The only good news was that she rarely felt the obligation to sleep next to him because he was usually too messed up to care. Still, she found it hard to talk to anyone besides Nathan because the original crew was in search of the old times, unable to shake their growing addictions.

Nikki saw a different side of Billy than the one she'd had so much fun with early on. He was noticeably depressed and often incoherent. He'd ramble long into the night, bragging about his conquests, lofty talents, and vague intentions of changing the world. The further in he fell, the more he felt the need to gain attention from anyone who would listen, as his closest friends ceased to take him seriously. Yet, every now and then there was that touch of genius, an instant of powerful clarity, a few charming phrases of wisdom amid the most miserable moments of his demise. Sometimes Nikki would find him curled up in the corner of the deck, vomiting over the railing until blood and black bile dripped from his chin. He would stare up from his land of the lost, smile with stained teeth, and say, "Don't worry honey, I'm ok. Just doing research is all, finding out what we're really made of. It'll all turn out, it'll be the way I planned, I promise."

Although nothing could diminish the joy Nathan held each day, he began to feel sorry for his bewildered friend and occasionally slipped back into those old patterns of self-destruction. He may have even been enjoying the fresh status of hanging out with his girl's ex-lover.

Kerby was the first to see the blissful duality in Nathan's eyes. One night, he called out his young apprentice on his perplexed state of happiness, so Nathan confided in him all the glorious details. The wise captain smiled with disbelief, then warned him to be careful with the powder keg of Billy's buried emotions. "That boy's not well," he concluded, "and news like this might just tip him over the edge of sanity. So you be careful, I don't wanna see anyone dead because of shits and giggles."

Nathan took the advice seriously. He tried to be careful with his game of chance by getting ever closer to Billy. It was easy to fall back into the stormy life because this time he was enjoying every minute of it. But gradually, when jolting substances were running through his veins, he took more risks to be with Nikki. Yes, the freedom of unlimited pleasure and the ecstasy of secret romance drove him to new levels of carelessness. Slowly, the noose of corruption began to wrap itself more firmly around the trio, awaiting a chance to hang them for their thoughtless exploitation of the finer things in life.

It was around this time when Billy began to fixate on Nikki. He must have sensed her widening distance or roiling temptation because he suddenly found reason to be exclusive with her. Once or twice, while the three of them were hanging out together in the early hours, the despondent gentleman talked of marriage and kids. Of course, Nikki just winked Nathan's way because they both knew it was the desperate pipedream of a lost man.

The rope got a bit tighter for the couple when Garo walked in on them in the recording studio one night as they embraced in the candlelight. Billy was right behind, so Garo made an about face and pushed him back towards the game room. He was good at keeping a secret so the couple laughed it off and continued to record while in the buff. However, a few days later one of Billy's contending hussies, (the crew called her Sundown Stephanie) stumbled onto deck, pulled her panties to the side to take a leak over the railing, and spotted them lying together under a table. There was nothing to do to avoid the noose as it clenched their necks with its prickly fingers.

That evening, Nikki looked on as Stephanie used the information to her advantage, monopolizing Billy's attention. Nikki sought out Nathan and they watched intently, trying to get a hint of what the slut was whispering in his ear. As they stared through the glare of the setting sun, they saw Billy shake his head and hide his face in his hands. Horrified, the couple snuck off and waited for their fall for the better part of two days and nights.

But when Billy finally approached, they discovered that the one constant on the ship was that he was becoming more and more unpredictable.

He sat down on the edge of Nikki's lounge chair looking vulnerable and shaken. Then, he brought up the rumor that they'd been recording together in the studio and said he wanted to be a part of their creative surge. Taken aback, they stared ahead without a word until he pleaded like a lost animal, claiming he only wanted to play with them again. Nikki recognized a chance to make a break for Nathan and motioned him forward with her easy glare.

Given little choice, Nathan followed Garo downstairs; afraid he'd be forced to record intimate love songs with his keeper. The awkward session began when Billy broke out a bottle of Dom and led a toast with his talented inner circle. For the first time in ages, the original gang was together doing their thing. Garo spread his instruments across the floor, excited to get a fresh chance at their old sound. Charge sat on a couch with both arms slung around dreadful women, bobbing his head to the rising beat. And Billy passed around samples of his chemical courage, fiendishly trying to pull his friends into his devastating world. Nathan took a deep breath and decided to have fun with the whole thing.

Soon, requests from the Beatles, Zeppelin, U2, Marley and a multitude of others came in, and he was up for them all. He was in prime form, letting loose with the same icy elegance as Cobain's unplugged masterpiece. His voice was strong, deep, clear, sharp, a twang from the south shaken up with Motown and mixed with a distinct island flavor, at the same time fluid, striking, masculine. Impressions of lyrics and flashes of poems began to come to him with abounding clarity, the source of inspiration centering on his passions for Nikki. As he looked around at the lost faces trying to come together, it all became just another part of the game. He watched Nikki sitting next to him on Billy's lap, and discovered a way to pour out his feelings in love-induced code, creating mysterious symbolism to release his prevailing feelings.

It was clear how talented he was at improvisation, deliberately revealing partial secrets that dwelled at the base of her soul. Riding his talent, the gang played all night and into the morning, rolling together in waves of insight, breaking down barriers of musical influence, beginning their liquid movement. Beyond question, he took them somewhere else, somewhere they really wanted to be, thought they were, or wished they could get to.

Of course, Nikki was the only one who understood Nathan's ingenious play on words. The more he revealed the furtive details of their relationship, the more she began to get off on his double meanings. She could barely stand the warm rivers of passion running under the glacial surface of his lyrics. And as soon as the others left, they made passionate love right in front of Billy, who'd rolled off his chair and passed out on the floor while still holding his guitar.

By the next morning, guilt had risen to a feverish level in Nikki's mind. As stimulating as the experience had been, she realized that she couldn't take another day of the bound-up stress. She urged Nathan awake and spoke for fifteen minutes straight, explaining that things would have to change. "Nathan, my sweet," she finally found the courage to admit, "we're going to have to tell Billy."

He shook his head and rolled over in bed, peering out at the blue slit of sky from his tiny porthole. She nuzzled in closer and continued, "Come on Nathan, we can't live like this until the end of our days. You know what we have to do."

He turned back towards her and said, "I know." Deep down he understood that they were being hurtful to someone who had given them so much.

She continued, "Seriously, it's not fair to any of us."

"Nikki, I understand, believe me. I don't know what else to say other than you've been my saving grace. But I love letting loose and I enjoy these wild times. I'm not sure I'm ready to give it all up."

"So what are you saying?"

"I'm saying I like how things are right now. So, just a little longer, Nikki, that's all. Let me get all of this out of my system."

A flush of apprehension filled her cheeks. "Why do you need to live like this?"

"Because for the first time in my life, I have it all."

She grabbed his chin and stroked his morning stubble. "Don't you understand, we have it all when we're together."

"I know, but it's hard to say goodbye to living on both sides of the coin."

"Aren't you being a tad selfish? I know he's not the most decent bloke in the world, but he's done a lot for us. And I don't want to see him suffer any more than he already is."

"Then why should we tell him? Will it make him feel any better?"

Her inspiration and passion continued to swell in the tranquil hours. "Because I'm ready to make right in my world. The thing is, you've helped me see the light. You've shown me everything I want out of life, and I'm ready to get on with this dream. So I ask you, are you set to begin a new adventure, full of good choices?"

"I'm ready to do whatever will make us happy."

She wrapped her arms around him and squeezed. "Then tell me, what do ya' want to do next?" This was Nikki's way of letting him know it was time to move on.

He looked up to the ceiling, his fading morning buzz tossing his mind into a spin. She pressed the issue with her sexy stare. "Honestly, I'm worried about ya mate, there are ways to get that good feeling other than going off the deep end with the rest of these dags. Come on with ya, you're the one who tells me we have the world by the balls. So other than getting smashed every other night, what d'ya wanna do?"

He joked back, "I'd like to get lost in the jungle with you and make mad love through the darkest hours."

He tried to laugh, but she just stared deeper into his eyes and said, "Luv, I'm serious. I need to get away from here for a while, more than just our secret mornings or our day trips. We deserve some time alone to think things out."

Nathan suddenly understood they were losing that perfect shine that so delicately encases a new relationship. This burst of reality compelled him to give in to her. "You're right, we should run away to one of those little islands we passed a ways back and get lost for a few days. Rough it a bit so we grasp the spirit of our animation." Warming to the idea, he continued, "Let all this chaos go, give in to our temptation, and let the gods sort it out."

151

A deep sigh eased from Nikki's diaphragm. "Thank you, this will be good for us. And if Billy doesn't realize something's amiss after two or three days, we'll tell him when we get back."

Nathan didn't agree, but he went along with her to secure the moment.


Later that day, Nikki sought out Kerby and pleaded with him to hang loose, to inconspicuously circle the area until their return. He agreed, but wouldn't let her leave before giving her his flawless words of wisdom. "You read Hemmingway much?" he asked. She shook her head so he called her in closer and said, "Well, don't bother because they're living through him for ya." She looked confused until he added, "I don't know what you're after, but you best be careful 'cause those two bulls are charging blindly at one another and you're the thin red cape dancing in the middle."

Nikki was up most of the night, pondering the significance of Kerby's haunting words. She woke Nathan before dawn. They loaded the Zodiac with a cooler, scuba gear, and a few boards and headed out in search of their escape.

After some lucky navigating, Nathan found an isolated chain of islands cut out of tropical fantasy off the Flores Coast. They approached the beachhead and noticed the main landmass was really split into two islands, separated by an immaculate, turquoise-clear lagoon. When the Zodiac came to rest on the unspoiled shoreline underlining the perfect contrast of white sands and emerald peaks, Nathan knew that Nikki had been right.

Anticipation buzzed in his brain and excitement jumped through his loins as he sprang off the boat like a nutty kid and began to scout the landscape. Truly, he craved this liberty; his penetrating nature yearned for a last chance to explore every square inch of virgin territory before the adult world could cut him off forever from the seeds of actualization. He grabbed Nikki's hand and they waded across the shallows to the interior island, an eroded cone with green crags guarding a deep woodland valley in the center. Before the couple broke through the threshold of shadows, belligerent calls from the jungle interior told them that the islands were teeming with wildlife.

Nathan paused to listen and a child-like grin spread over his features, for seldom in life does one genuinely feel alive at a fundamental level for extended periods of time. While the couple became immersed in the sheer cliffs and overhanging plant life that seemed to be swaying in place in the midst of the flowing walls of water, the essential elements of existence focused in around them. Every absorbing step was a gateway into a hypnotic state of insight, charging him forward through primordial fear with a lust for excitement and mystery. Yes, his eternal will had returned. Years later, Nathan would realize they had explored some of the same caves that a dwarf-like species of hominids were discovered in, a missing link in the evolutionary chain that would take the science world by storm.

For hours, they became a part of the jungle floor, welcoming the cornucopia of plush birds in the region, as Java kingfishers, yellow-throated parrots, green-naped lorikeets, and wrinkled hornbills bobbed out from tangled tress and sometimes peaked into view of Nikki's lens. Outlandish monkeys swung out from green shadows to catch a curious glimpse of the foreigners, demonstrating little fear due to limited interaction. As the couple grew more and more absorbed in the sounds of nature's song, displays of audacious acrobatics, and splashes of brilliant color, they were inspired to record the rhythmic jungle clamor for future works. Nikki was right, Nathan thought, the only way to true happiness was by following her vision of *self-construction.*

As he took it all in, he grew doubly pleased because he saw the physical burdens of stress leaving Nikki's features once again. Nothing made him happier than watching his beautiful mate ease into her true self and share her absolute lust for life with the planet. She was at home while surrounded by the striking birds and mischievous monkeys, lending credence to her exotic eyes and alluring nature. Once again he began to envision her blissful destiny, the incredible difference she would make in her lifetime. Encapsulated moments from the expedition would simmer in his hot pipe as the most cherished memories during the dark years to come.

Those four days were extraordinary, a time to feel the verve, to heal past wounds, and open to new possibilities. Together, they realized that there was little need for words because they were sharing the same thoughts, reveling in the same unspoken truth. It didn't matter whether they were hiking concealed trails, surfing uncharted breaks, interacting with rare animals, staring into comforting flames, or making mad love in the moonlight, they were alive, absorbed in the rightful reality, effortlessly a part of it all.

Since the onset of their relationship, their heightened connection to source had fostered a natural magnetism that led to incredible encounters with the wild side. It was as if God's creatures somehow understood and trusted their union of divine energy, and were curious to be a part of it. More and more often when they were alone together, they found themselves in outlandish situations with diverse creatures. Nathan welcomed the contact like a politician welcomes an eager crowd. Nikki began to log humorous stories about overly friendly insects, arrogant florescent lizards, large lonesome rodents, sexually promiscuous primates, and kleptomaniac crabs.

As much as he liked exploring the jungle landscape, his connection with the ocean never felt so strong. It didn't matter what activity he was involved in, he continuously felt the vivid vitality of the ever-changing surface. But sharing the experience of diving with Nikki was especially powerful. As they plummeted into the rich depths, he felt the life in the water's structure, the delicate balance of conservation and change in the oodles of rare species. Gliding spellbound in the world underwater, he perceived how strange evolutionary tracks fit together to create the incredible diversity in shape, features, and color. Bizarre fish told stories of God's genius, some with foot-like fins for walking on the ocean floor, others with seaweed-like camouflage blending them into the foliage.

Much of the time Nikki preferred to hang out on her paddleboard, observing her man in action. Watching Nathan play with sea animals was like watching a little boy unwrap his most cherished Christmas gift. Nikki caught dynamic photographs of him

155

riding the fins of majestic manta rays, dancing in slow motion with green sea turtles, swimming in the middle of schools of reef sharks, and kissing the forehead of a moray eel. A few weeks back, she had captured an incredible series of shots as a pod of eight dolphins rode a wave with him, their smiling bottlenoses streaming through the sapphire water like friendly torpedoes as he followed their line.

Of course, not all his interactions with ocean life were welcoming, as some terrifying moments with the cold-blooded creatures had made a lasting impression. One time off the coast of Australia, a school of frenzied sharks had scouted the area around the thin line of surfers, displaying their vertical fins as a warning that the session was over. When it happened again near Tasmania, Nathan began splashing the surface in frustration as he boarded the Zodiac, and one of the predators bumped him with its sharp fin, slicing a three-inch gash in his midsection. Another time, while surfing in the Coral Islands, Nathan leapt off a wave and his foot went right through the spherical interior of a jellyfish. The blue blob's flimsy tentacles wrapped around his ankle and made pink track marks up his leg that throbbed with pain for nights on end. However, the scare Nathan and Nikki got on their third day alone on the deserted island was off the charts as far as close calls go.

Certain tales may be told to perfection, their narrator using just the right words to paint a colorful picture for the mind's eye, yet never fully appreciated, or even believed. This is one of those rare stories. So, if you can't quite grasp the power of the animal that set its sites on the vulnerable couple that early evening, pause for a second to consider how it must have felt to be out there, alone, staring at the worst kind of death.

The sun was a glowing bulb hanging low in the sky as the lovers floated on immaculate waters, waiting for one more set before heading to their beach camp. A few large seabirds had left their island outcrop and were hanging out around the breakpoint. The one closest to them was particularly anxious, flapping sporadically and barking muffled caws as if it had warning something was wrong. Nathan wondered why it didn't just fly away, and a few times he shooed it with splashes of water. There was a moment of dead calm, an extended lull, and a rising sense of relief in the bird's pink eyes.

But just as Nathan pointed to a massive shadow coming up from the depths, the surface exploded in an almost perfect black circle. Twisting out of the water was a young killer whale, flashing his brilliant pattern of shiny charcoal and white. He picked off the stunned gull no more than ten yards beyond the break. The reckless calf then darted straight down under Nathan's board, leaving nothing but a trail of feathers. The couple could do little more than look at each other, laughing in amazement. Orcas are rare in the warm waters of the South Pacific, and Nathan's first thought was that the whale had been separated from his pod while looking for food. A minute later, the jovial bloke surfaced, and as he made an inquisitive pass Nathan was able to rub his glossy black skin with delicate fingers. Nikki clicked a few frames before the lone whale again disappeared from sight.

The lovers had centered their attention on the energetic calf, but were unaware that a desperate mother was in search of her

157

youngster. What happened next was the most amazing natural encounter they would ever witness. Appearing from nowhere, the matriarch burst out of the water with a full breach, her glistening flank sending a wall of water over Nathan, nearly knocking him off of his board. The massive mom then withdrew down under and came up again between the human and the calf, cutting her son off from any further danger. As her glowering eyes turned toward Nathan, white mask concealing instinctive intentions, she seemed to pause and ponder for a moment, thinking through her final decision.

In the next instant, she was charging him with mouth agape, six thousand pounds of muscle jetting forward without regard. For a split second Nathan was on the bottom of the food chain, realizing the trepidation of being eaten alive, identifying with every form of prey that had ever been consumed. Her broad tongue and yellowing teeth became his solitary focus, the cavernous point of impact growing larger and more menacing as he envisioned the sensation of being tossed around like a seal pup and ripped apart limb from limb.

He should have been terrified, but grew utterly calm. In fact, he was almost enjoying her majesty, unable to think of anything other than the idea that there was no better way to die. The intensity of those seconds was something Nathan would never forget, for he saw the legend of Ahab in her eyes. But somewhere along the way she regained her wits, and a moment before impact she let up and veered left. It was her boy who changed her mind. He had surfaced right in front of Nathan and let fly a short burst of high-pitched squeals, unwilling to give up his new plaything.

Nature has a funny way about her sometimes, and at this point the encounter meandered past the limit of logical comprehension. With bobbing head and gesturing fins, the calf seemed to motion Nathan to play with him. And after raising his hands to big momma as if to ask permission, that's exactly what Nathan did. For a few precious moments he was in the water swimming side by side with mother and child.

Nikki sat spellbound on her board, watching the love of her life become a temporary extension of the cetacean family. She saw the magic with her own eyes, and no scientist or minister could take that away from her. In her mind, the mystery of the natural world had come together, not in ancient artifacts revealed or primeval codes broken, but with the silent brilliance of understanding. She saw that it is the unique individuals, those exceptional mammals willing to break through the limits of hardwired genetics, that are able to change the interpretation of the universe.

Late that night, as they sat at the campfire reflecting upon everything that happened, Nikki began talking strangely about the unworldly experience. With flickering flames distorting her features, she claimed it felt as if the baby whale had spoken to her, warning them to get off the ship. Nathan listened intently, then laughed it off, pouring her another glass of wine before drifting to sleep. But his dreams told him that she was right, something larger and more powerful was leading him to his destiny.

Early the next morning, they decided to head back to the ship and face the inevitable.

## 13

Billy was waiting for the lovers as they boarded the *Rumrunner*, the streak of restlessness in his glare heightening their anxiety. Before they could set foot on deck or even say a word, he'd cornered them, his wild eyes trying to focus while lively ideas bubbled from a newly tapped well of enthusiasm. It was clear Billy had done some soul searching while they were gone because things were noticeably different on the ship. Most significantly, the vessel had been cleansed of its spirit-sucking rabble because he'd dropped the lot of them off at the nearest port.

After the couple had caught their breath, Billy called a meeting of his inner circle. Soon, his estranged companions were gathered at the outdoor bar, wondering what was on his frantic mind. He made one of his customary toasts to his each of buddies, thanking them for the magnificent times they'd shared. Then he lifted his champagne glass to Nathan and Nikki and said, "I know things have been kind'a crazy around here, and I thank you for giving me my wake up call. See, when the two of you went away, I did some thinking because I lost the two of ya once and I don't' want it to happen again."

He paused and addressed them all, speaking with his former charm and animation. "Listen, everyone knows I've been an asshole lately. I realize things are breaking up and I don't want all this to end the way I fear it might. So before I go broke or jump off this ship and try to swim back to the way things used to be, I'd like to have one more run together. You see, we all need to find ourselves in our own terms and I think I found a way to do that."

Garo interrupted, "Straight up. But what's wrong with the way things are? Weren't we in the groove the other night?"

"Yah, but it's just that I need some answers in life because they're not coming to me like I dreamed. Honestly, when it's all said and done, I'd like to think I did something important. We all want that, and when I'm liquored up, I talk about it with some of you. But it never goes anywhere. So I thought, what better way to strip down to the bare bones than a journey into the unknown to find our calling on this earth."

Charge, feeling the first glimpse of that vacant hangover that would become his future, answered for the group. "Sounds tight, but we've been here before. So how do you think we're gonna get *there* at this point? Hell, we barely even surf anymore."

"I'm glad you asked, my friend, because I've uncovered our ticket to a new adventure." Billy took a moment to go below deck and returned with a delicate Indonesian woman who'd only been on the ship a few days. "Fellows, I'd like you all to meet Kade."

A new face was no surprise to the group at this point. But for whatever reason, young Kade was the center of his newly found passion with her distinctive body and interesting personality. Nikki intuitively perceived the shallow soul in the woman, someone who knew the meaning of no good. Her sharp cheeks and full lips were attractive enough, but they hid a luring undercurrent of conspiracy.

As Billy rambled on, Nikki could hear how his essence burned with the fires of repentance. "My search for truth has left me empty and broken. There are places in this world and in my mind that I've only dreamed of exploring. But Kade here has connections that will allow us to look over that ledge of existence. That mysterious view that we all long to catch a glimpse of." The odd-looking woman next to him smiled slyly as he continued, "This fine young lady knows the location of an isolated tribe of the Mentawai that lives in the islands off Sumatra. Many of their people have been forced to adapt because of pressures from the outside, but this group has gone deeper into the forest to hide their secrets and continue their way of life. And what a life it is. Their shamans have medicines that can let us enter other worlds. I'm not kidding, she says they can take us into the depths of the universal soul, help us to communicate with our lower selves. So I propose we stay with these people for a stretch and see what they can teach us. Learn their ways, share their secrets, and hopefully come out with a fresh perspective. And when we return, we'll be ready to jump into our true desires."

Nikki began to feel sorry for him and looked towards Nathan for answers, but he just stared down at the deck with an adventurous smirk on his lips. She was also intrigued, but asked Billy, "Why would she show us this hidden tribe?"

"Well, Kade explained to me that the Mentawai way of life is in serious trouble. There are agencies that are trying to save these people but there are others that are exploiting the hell out of them. They need help, that's for sure. I'm paying her a lot of money of course, and she'll use the money to help their cause."

Nikki was indignant when she said, "It seems like we'll be invading their territory. I don't think they need a bunch of tourists crashing in on their scene." Yet the sociologist deep inside longed for such an incredible cultural experience.

Billy used his larger-than-life charisma to help her see it his way. "Think about it Nikki, we've talked so much about getting real, and this is our chance. I mean how many times will you ever get the chance to live in the shadow of the primeval?"

With the rest of the gang on board, Nikki conceded. As the group came together with excited laughter, Billy was delighted because he'd again discovered a way to be the ringmaster, that self-proclaimed hero. Cheers were heard again on the *Rumrunner* when Billy ordered Kerby to change course. No one seemed to notice when the captain called back from his post with a bogus accent, "Yes Sir, Mista' Kurtz."

Nathan couldn't help but grinning to himself with a shameful contempt that throbbed from Kerby's masterful use of words. Nathan knew it was a bad idea, felt the hypocrisy in the whole lifestyle, and perceived the trouble headed for them like a four hundred ton ship. But, like the others, he just couldn't shake the captivating addiction that was Billy Windsor. He would ride his friend's dangerous antics and once-in-a-lifetime opportunities right over the falls.

Late that night, Nathan whispered his concerns to Nikki while hiding under silky sheets. After some hesitation, he said, "Nikki, I know you want to leave, but I'm having a hard time deciding what to do next. As fucked up as Billy can be, he sure

163

keeps things interesting. Now I told you we'd get off, and if that's what you really want to do, then tell me now and we're as good as gone."

She surprised him when she nodded in agreement. "It's true, the bloke sure knows how to rise from his own ashes. And I can't ask for a more incredible opportunity." She paused and Nathan saw a flash of ire in her eyes. "Sure he's dodgier than a sausage in a finger stall, but I think we might be the only fools on God's green earth that can help him."

"You think he's really capable of change?"

"I can't put an answer on that, but there's something to it. What's it that makes you keep comin' back for more? I mean, he's been a pretty dirty bastard to you too on occasion, but you seem to wanna keep hanging around. It's because he makes you feel alive, isn't it?"

Nathan laid his head on her golden-brown breasts and began to think things through. It was hard to explain, but Billy had some intangible quality, a numinous influence that allowed people to love him despite himself. Even when he was stabbing you in the back, you were secretly rooting him on. *But why?*

The answer that kept circling his mind had something to do with Billy's infamous Midway adventure. Early on in their journey, Billy had become enamored with Nathan's candor and depth. He may have teased and harassed him in front of the party crowd, but while they were alone he'd confide in him night after night. It was in those moments when he took Nathan under his wing, unveiled his

164

infinite gift like a smooth encyclopedia salesman or a slick drug dealer. Nathan pulled Nikki in close and tried to express his interpretation of that double-edged power. He began, "Well, the last time I heard him talk like this was on the Midway Islands, before I met you."

She seemed interested, so he continued to softly spin the tale of how he had fallen in love with the legend of Billy Windsor. The journey began after their last evening surfing in the Hawaiian Islands, when Billy took over the wheel, turned away from their southern jaunt towards Australia to head northwest in search of the illusive *trooper spirit*, as he called it. The crazed man was vague about his true intent, but Nathan was just happy to gain a sense of acceptance after showing off his weak surf skills on the North Shore of Oahu.

Billy kept strict company with Nathan throughout the unintended trip, harping on the idea that it was something he needed to do, yet unwilling to tell anyone where they were headed. The striking thing was it was the first time Nathan saw that surfing was nothing more than a cool diversion, a dreamy escape, from Billy's comprehensive plan. While they drank the days away on the bridge, the fascinating man confided countless stories about historic battles of the past, shared astonishing views of social reformation, laughed at his eclectic list of the greatest historic figures, and lit up intimate dreams for the world's future.

Then, about 180 miles north of the Midway Islands, Billy grew grave and serious. He silenced the engines, walked over to the deck rail and began to illustrate the details of the Battle of Midway.

165

As he described the full account of how each of the four Japanese and one American aircraft carriers had come to lie at rest thousands of feet below, he made Nathan close his eyes and visualize the faces of the Americans who lost their lives that day. Nathan began to understand the power of a great storyteller as he could nearly see the ghosts from the *U.S.S. Yorktown's* mangled iron fortress resting in the unforgiving darkness. But Nathan opened his eyes again to the empty blue sea when he heard Billy say, "But I wouldn't have had the balls to do what those men did."

Nathan asked, "What do ya mean?"

It was then that Billy opened to his insecurities and narrowed in on his life mission. "You know, lose my life for my country, other people's beliefs. Could you imagine flying in one of those steel blue sardine cans, only eighteen or nineteen years old, ditching and dodging the Jap's fire, hot lead diggin' into your back?" His companion shook his head while Billy continued, "See, what bothers me is I'll never be a hero, yet that's all I ever wanted to be. And there's nothing I can do that would stack up to what they did out there."

Nikki sat wide-eyed on the bed, remembering (though a bit uneasily) why she had fallen for Billy Windsor. Nathan then discussed their experiences on the Midway Islands, the abandoned pillboxes, the empty beaches, and the ominous scrap metal. The setting was so romantic, a living war museum on a grander scale than Pearl Harbor, that Nikki might have heard the buzz of enemy aircraft overhead. Nathan described how the nearly deserted airbase, a speck of beach in the Pacific that had been the turning point of

166

World War II, was now nothing more than a sanctuary for hundreds of thousands of birds. He explained how Billy was reeking of nostalgia on that day, talking rapidly as if he'd been there many times before, while the rest of the crew could say little, other than ask what kind of waves could possibly break on the sandy little atoll. Soon, the jokes dried up and faces turned grim because it was clear that Billy was on a mission, possessed by his hereditary demons.

Billy took Nathan for a high-speed ride in the Zodiac, roaring under what had been the hot spot in the air until he suddenly cut the engine in a deep lagoon on the west side of Sand Island. There, they explored the perimeter for a time, using sonar to view various geometric forms at moderate depths. Then, while leaning over the rubber pontoon, Billy scrunched his face to the horizon and pointed to a flinking fuselage in the shallows.

Minutes later they were secure in their scuba gear, thirty feet underwater. He'd somehow paid off a few of the soldiers to let him dive the main wreckage field. In the stark silence of the liquid graveyard, they explored the Dauntless dive-bomber partially sunk in the sand. The plane's mounted machine gun was cracked in half, but still seemed to be blazing with memories of fire at a passing school of silverfish. Deeper down the line was a Wildcat and a Japanese Zero, their props nearly intertwined in the final place of rest. The two companions glided upon the site for closer inspection, and Nathan was overcome with a sense of living history, as if God had pressed the pause button on this part of the world for the past fifty years. The awed men inspected the planes carefully, studying cracked windshields, circular bullet holes in tails and wings, and the daring octopus that had made a home in the cockpit of the Zero. Then Billy spotted the perfect piece of memorabilia and spent ten minutes prying out a round that had somehow become lodged in the iron works of the Zero's machine gun.

When they surfaced, Billy held up the warbled bullet and said, "This is what's been missing from my life, and now it belongs to me." Nathan blew off the comment, assuming his buddy was after another unique souvenir to add to his exotic collection. But Billy would drill a hole in the bullet and wear it around his neck for the rest of his life. It wasn't until months later when Kerby opened him to his friend's rich family history that Nathan realized the trip to Midway was really about something more. It seems that Billy's only hero, his larger-than-life grandfather who he had modeled his life after, had piloted a Wildcat that had been shot down by overwhelming Japanese fire power while defending the airbase early in the battle. As a child, he'd made his idol repeatedly tell the full version of the disturbing tale, solidifying in his mind the exact details of the dogfight leading up to the crash. And for all he knew, it might have even been his grandfather's plane they had explored under the depths of time.

While sitting in bed with Nikki, on the ship that was named after a man greater than them both, Nathan finally understood why he needed yet another journey with his friend. For all of Billy's faults, he was ingenious, full of life, and exciting. He thought about the talk Billy had had with him before they left Midway that morning. Back then Nathan could do little more than listen, unnerved by the man's clandestine intensity, but now the speech made total sense. He had spoken from the heart with the recklessness of a frothing mastermind. "Think about what it must have been like to go down in flames before living life." He paused, then bellowed, "Hell, for some of them, before even getting their dick's wet. Those are the real heroes man, no one else can compare. What do we have today that compares? Fame? Status? I could have that. But it's nothing, no matter what I do. I don't want to be famous any more than I want to be dead. But I need more, I need to prove something, do something, for this fucked up world. I have thoughts and ideas and dreams inside me that I hope are a fraction as great as those men were. And I want to give my hopes to this world so those men can rest in peace, knowing they died for the right cause." He paused and gave Nathan the most vulnerable look he'd ever seen. "Listen, we could do it together. Create something big, my brother. I want the world to understand things, recognize man's sacrifice."

It was all so overwhelming, so irresistible, it was the reason he'd fallen in love with Billy Windsor. The idea that his guide wanted to make Nathan a part of something extraordinary dotted the *i's* and crossed the *t's* in Nathan's soul. This empty promise, this unfulfilled dream, this sure thing, was the carrot that drove him on through the endless highs and lows. And although Billy's inspiring talks had dried up in the riverbed of autumn addiction, Nathan held on to hope that his mentor would one day lead him to the promised land of revolution and transformation. He just didn't realize that he'd have to go at it alone.

Nikki interrupted his thoughts, "Nathan, I just don't see how going into the forest chasing nomads helps you get a break for your music career or gives us the opportunity to make a difference in this world. It seems like we're just wasting time…"

Nathan focused on Nikki's dark pupils and said, "I think Billy's trying to clean up and find himself. This is the first step; I just know it's the first step. And I think we need him as much as he needs us."

Nikki nodded, "You may be right. I see that he helps you spill out your latent passions. And his lifestyle constantly reminds you to what you really love. But what if you're wrong? What if it's just another of Billy's games?"

"I hear you. But a part of me is honored that he's chosen us to be part of something." He flashed his sheepish smile, "And anyway Nikki, I think he knows about us and doesn't care."

She smiled and shot back, "I think he knows about us and you don't care."

He laughed shyly, "Well, maybe."

"Don't worry, I don't think we need to complicate things anymore by telling him anything about us. We'll just wait until the time is right. In the meantime, let's see what more we can learn and see if we can talk him into helping you get an album together."

Nathan looked out the porthole at a faint landmass. "Nikki, things are changing. I feel it in my heart and soul."

## 14

As the ship cut through the Strait of Selat Sundra, the couple spent most of their time alone. Nathan showed Nikki the view from his high perch so she could enjoy the birdlike freedom and capture some of the fleeting landscapes on film. From there, they let the hours melt away while talking, thinking, and listening to the wind. They were no longer concerned about hiding their time together, although they were conscious about limiting public displays of affection.

Before first light on the third day at sea, their eyes began to peel away the misty corners of nautical glare, revealing the unspoiled Sumatra coastline. In degrees, the dense landscape appeared in dazzling color, outlining hints of splendid islands and peninsulas. Heading north along the western coast to the islands of the Mentawai, they had plenty of time for taking in the views. For hours they passed nothing but tangled thickets and blackened jungles, until they finally came upon the first signs of human habitation.

While cruising past the coastal slums of Padang, they noticed dark, skinny children waving to them from stilt shacks resting on the calm waters. Nikki was overcome with a deep sense of empathy. Minutes later they spotted the town center from the crow's nest and glimpsed bustling markets streaked with rich and multicolored vegetables. From the distance the villages appeared beautiful, but Nathan was glad to be watching the third world splendor from his own skin. He had an ominous feeling, an undefined hopelessness, because deep down he knew most of those children had little chance in life.

By noon, the exotic islands of the Mentawai came into full view. As Billy's excitement bubbled over, he crammed a week's worth of supplies into the Zodiac and hopped in with Kade, Nathan, Nikki, Charge and Garo. After a jam-packed ride to a batch of small huts tucked into an overgrown beach, Kade found the narrow trail that would lead them to their only human lifeline through the next stretch of deadly terrain. There, they met their contact, a teenage Mentawai who called herself Suku. The girl's russet skin, thin-lined tattoos, and attentive breasts immediately drew in the guys' attention.

After Kade slipped Suku a fistful of coins, they disappeared with Billy back to the Zodiac and didn't return until the next morning. The threesome went to Padang to purchase vital materials that the girl could trade with her people in return for the group's safe visit. Nathan, Nikki, and the guys spent the night huddled by a small fire, fending off endless formations of monstrous mosquitoes. The next morning, after they'd figured out the dynamics of the tradeoff, Nathan and Nikki were interested to find out what their lives were worth. Suku had purchased mostly raw metal, but she was also loaded up with a shallow iron caldron, a few machetes, an array of beads, and a horde of lighters.

They were quick to secure their gear and set off on the intense hike awaiting them. From the start, Nikki noticed Suku's scarred inner self, and was pleasantly surprised when she discovered the girl spoke a touch of English. As the tough little warrior guided

172

them along near impenetrable trails, Nikki struck up a friendship with her. With her untamed accent laced with mystical whispers, Suku explained how she'd been educated in the city of Padang because Christian missionaries had convinced her parents that a Western education would give her a better chance in life. However, the civilized world had done nothing less than stomp on her soul, as she found few opportunities in the city and was rejected by her own people when she returned home. She explained how she was currently splitting time between residing in the streets of the ghetto and living as an outcast member of her tribe, a messenger between the ancient world and encroaching modernization. But Nikki saw her for what she was, a discarded trinket, a failed test in a culture that was transitioning into extinction.

Suku's backcountry wisdom helped Nikki enjoy the half-day hike through the center of the tough, verdant land. The displaced girl was at home in the thick plant life, always the first to spot the multitude of creatures peeking out from the seams of bushes and creases in the trees. Despite her failures at *traditional learning*, Nikki was amazed at just how gifted she was in the art of connecting with the natural world. The gang might have felt like a team of celebrated naturalists as Suku pointed out striking silhouettes of Kloss gibbons, civet cats, snub-nosed monkeys, and short-tailed macaques. With such an exceptional woman by her side, Nikki began to feel the fragile power of the Mentawai culture in motion.

Yet, as a steady rain began to drizzle on them, they were reminded how difficult life was in the shadows. With the spirit of Suku in mind, Nikki tried very hard to stay positive through the sticky heat, maddening mud, unrelenting insects, and suffocating humidity. Nothing can describe nature's thick dominance in the jungle, as aromatic stems repeatedly rebutted their machetes, fingering branches became entwined in their backpacks, and dribbling water seeped into every nook of their bodies. No matter how excited Nikki pretended to be, the slow trek through the lost world and into an ever-blackening abyss became infuriatingly challenging.

All her bottled frustration came to a head when her sopping feet went out from under her on a declining slope. She slid down into a narrow ravine and when she came to rest at the edge of a stream, her right ankle was lodged in a tangle of vine-like roots. As she moaning in pain, unable to move, Billy and Nathan led the rush down the slope to help her. But as they hacked her out of her trap, Nikki felt contempt for both her men for talking her into this ridiculous pursuit to find their fading youth. She lay there in agony, realizing just how twisted it was for the scheming Kade to take advantage of their naive guide for a few silver coins.

Although she was on the verge of losing her cool, she allowed the guys to carry her back up the incline to the trailhead. Her swollen and bleeding ankle was getting the best of her until Suku put a sticky dressing on it that immediately numbed the pain. The unnerving mishap and Suku's soothing remedy compelled Nikki to let down her guard, perpetuating the fierce events that were on the horizon.

Just when it seemed as if Nikki couldn't go another step in the tangled interior, she heard the sound of rushing water through the thriving vegetation. Suku found a hidden platform at the edge of the river with six elaborately dugout canoes waiting for them. So began another day and a half journey into the core of the primeval world.

Nikki insisted she ride with Suku so Nathan and Billy were forced to follow them at a safe distance like a couple of schoolboys. In time, they settled quite effortlessly into the patterns of the river. Yet, as they drifted along, Nathan noticed that his buddy kept glancing over at Nikki's glistening top half as she paddled along the brown current. It was clear that one of Billy's goals for the trip was to win her back into his favor. Of course the pig also caught a few quick glances of Suku's bare breasts.

With the dense beauty at a safe distance, the canoe trip became a time of relaxation and respite. The group floated under water-carved limestone gorges and past abandoned native villages. Once again the unrelenting noises in the thickets kept them entertained, filling their minds with limitless sensations and wonderings. Sometimes they even got a glimpse of the festivities to come as they watched monogamous leaf monkeys and graceful flying squirrels leaping in the tree tops from one side of the river to the other. As they grew closer to their destination, the anticipation grew to feverish levels, all of them speculating at how their lives would change from the magical encounter with the Mentawai.

It had been days since they'd seen another human being so it was a bit startling when Nathan spotted three dark figures in colorful sarongs leaping out from an intricate rope bridge into the brown waters. They were adolescent warriors from Suku's tribe. Upon surfacing, the boys made mocking calls and challenging shouts

175

towards the canoes. Their calls didn't make Nathan feel very well because they sounded more like a warning than a welcome. But the agile young men swam up the river with them for miles, leading their guests all way to the banks of their hidden village.

Very few subcultures in the world can claim an existence that is entirely free from outside influence, but this was one of those rare finds. The simple Mentawai village appeared in Nathan's vision like an exhibit at a museum. His initial glimpses were of A-framed roofs thatched with precision, and then blank eyes watching him without curiosity. He led the way towards the clearing and the first resident he approached was a shriveled woman with a severe face and sunken cheeks, wading through a flooded ditch with her finally crafted net. Nathan smiled her way and she flashed her jagged, sharpened teeth, making him twinge with horror.

Seconds later, a group of six or seven men flew out of the trees and charged them with flashing wild eyes, brandishing poison tipped spears, and hollering crazed syllables. Nathan went down like a lump and rolled into the fetal position, unable to believe that his life was going to end so bizarrely. He cringed while waiting for the hot puncturing pain, but felt nothing more than warm laughter. He looked up and saw some of the same boys who'd swam alongside their canoes grimacing down at him. The assault was nothing more than a planned posture to impress their guests, an eerie sort of welcome. But from that moment on, Nathan was wary about the whole situation, realizing just how far from the norm they'd wandered this time.

The crew spent the first hours watching the Mentawai in action, learning their daily routines, while the tribesmen went on about their business as if the strangers weren't even there. Without question, they were a beautiful people, lean, well built, agile, yet relentlessly ruled by their daily rituals. Billy and the boys followed a few log trails cut through the undergrowth and tried to observe various adults performing their duties. Their activities were interesting enough. They spent their time grinding sago wood, fishing in shallow streams, gathering medicinal plants, and farming hillside terraces.

But the guys were looking for something more from the experience, so they met up again in the evening to watch a teenage boy receiving an artistic rite of passage. Although highly illegal in Sumatra, his body became the canvasses and his feverish pain was his reward. A sikeirei, or shaman, held him down and sliced into his chest with long blackened needles, crafting tattoos that streaked from head to toe in long elongated arches. Of course, Billy couldn't stand to be on the outside looking in, so he bet Charge that he wouldn't have the balls to get something like that done. After trading a pouch full of beads he'd gotten from Kanak islanders, Billy watched in pleasure as the shaman joined three of Charge's previous tattoos with stylized black lines known as the Jarayak, or tree of life. Later, while Charge drank away his fever, he said that he'd rather be tortured or burned alive than again deal with such slow agony.

While the boys struggled to become men, Nikki sat alone in the uma house resting her ankle most of the day, taking in the view of a young woman caring for her infant son. Peeking through the foliage, she could not only see the affectionate mother, but also other clan members that visited to extend endless love, warmth, and lessons to the bright-eyed baby. In fact, the little ones seemed to be the center of the tribe, the focus of their liveliness. Nikki began to feel a sense of melancholy, wondering if she could ever find such a simple balance in the years to come.

Growing restless, she got up and limped over to Suku's shelter. Nikki remained unobtrusive as she watched from a distance, but was pleased at how the frail father had welcomed the girl back to his home. The sparkle in her friend's eye caused Nikki to tear up, and for a few minutes she felt there was a worthwhile reason for coming. It was hard to describe her commitment to humanity, for she believed she was chosen to lead each lost individual back from quenched hopes. As she viewed the proud woman chatter on about memories of better times, Nikki wondered if the elders could be convinced to allow their lost princess to return for good.

Yet, despite the amazing lessons in human compassion, the reality of being thrown into an archaic culture was something for which the crew had not prepared. From the onset, they felt a sense of awkwardness and helplessness, as they didn't know what to do with themselves during the eternal rituals. Without modern medication, the clan was constantly fighting jungle disease with a plethora of magical remedies made from the surrounding roots, leaves, and flowers. Theirs was a life of desperation, supernatural relief, and unthinkable tragedy, a restless sea rolling back and forth from pure joy to devastating heartbreak. For the Mentawai, despite the strictest custom, death was always right around the corner.

Worst of all, the crew had little ability to communicate with the Mentawai. The mischievous Kade had quickly taken up shelter with a young warrior, slowly prying him away form his traditional lifestyle with promises of opportunity in the city, while the joyful Suku was spending all of her time with her estranged family. And the rest of the tribe didn't have the time to include their guests because they were too wrapped up in their life-saving ceremonies and dreadful taboos. Billy grew unnerved by their incessant nature, unable to charm them into liking him. Slowly, the group began to realize that their stay would not be the glorious, romantic beam of light that they had imagined, but rather a dim, grim ember casting a shadow on the realities of existence. Only Nikki saw the benefit in the idea of her friends learning these lessons the hard way.

By the fourth day, Billy had had enough backwoods living and was ready to slide back to the ship and get on his way. But when a young shaman spoke to him in gestures, demonstrating how there would be a ceremonial feast for the spirits that evening, Billy's hopes for discovering their secrets were renewed. This was the invitation they had been waiting for, the reason for attempting the demanding journey in the first place. The anticipation of glimpsing a dreamlike world grew, and the crew felt as if they were on their way to some sort of mysterious journey.

While taking a few moments alone, Nathan stumbled upon two elderly shamans who had a small pig pinned down in the mud. The thing winced and bucked, but could not escape their tight grip. Once the legs and snout were properly tied, the meditative men

179

began to rub enchanted leaves over the pig while repeating ghostly chants, apparently asking for forgiveness and positive karma from the spirits. Watching closely, Nathan learned how difficult and delicate a process it was for the Mentawai to kill a living being. They went out of their way to ensure as comfortable a death as possible, continually singing into its eyes with soothing hymns. But Nathan focused on the life force buried within the squealing animal and was struck by the insane panic in its eyes. When the shamans were satisfied with the signs, they placed the squiggling pig in the glowing pit and its high-pitched whines could be heard for miles. It was then that Nathan understood the ironic fear in the Mentawai. They were perpetually preparing for their own deaths.

For whatever reason, the build up to the enchantment allowed the crew to celebrate. A half hour before the young shaman signaled to them to head over to the ceremony, Billy opened his backpack and dumped out his secret stash of hard liquor, hashish, and magic mushrooms. Raising his eyebrows, he asked his friends, "Well, are all of you ready to go on the ride of your lives?"

Since their return from the tragedies in Bangladesh, Nathan and Nikki had remained relatively low-key in the party scene, spending most of their energy recuperating emotional strength rather than burying the displaced passion in the bottle. This was especially true for Nikki, who had been clean since the day of the hurricane. But her time of healing was coming to an end because she was looking for a sign. Feeling the dull pain throbbing in her ankle, she downed a few shots and hit the hash pipe one too many times.

By the time they were directed to the central uma, a communal house that had been forbidden to enter up until this point, obscure winds of expectancy were murmuring secrets into their acute ears. Four sikeireis were seated in a center circle, while other tribe members outlined the floor of the spacious room. There was a nervous energy inside, as if the Mentawai were afraid of breaking traditional taboos by having their guests become a part of such an important ceremony. Despite the concern, the whole group was already deep in hypnotic chants.

Nikki entered with polished eyes and immediately pointed at the row of adorned animal skulls that lined the lip of thatched walls. Ancestral pigs, deer, and monkeys looked down from circular eye sockets, while their sinister grins smiled with a hint of Golding's insight in their empty skulls. But the selfish desires of the Western world could not understand the sacred symbolism in such ornaments. Nathan watched with discomfort as Billy slyly wiggled a pointy tooth from the jaw-line of an ape and slipped it in the pocket of his haggard silk shirt.

Moments later, all eyes were locked on the sikeireis who were offering sacred alalapet leaves to the conquered prey of the past. A critical hunt was in order the next morning and the shamans needed to call upon the phantom primates to ensure a proper expedition. The tribal men, decorated in ornate leaves hanging from their heads and waists, began to speak to the thick, empty air with that ever-present fat cigarette dangling from their lips. Soon, they were in motion, multicolored blurs of activity reaching into the ancient times for guidance.

Flickering torches, shifty-dark corners, and unhinged human activity mixed with the sweeping hum in Nikki's mind to create a fascinating atmosphere. From the edge of her reality, she saw the flourishing lights merge with the interior connection of existence. She stared at the shaman's rising movements and alluring gestures; it was as if a strand of wound prophecy was playing out in her head. Ideas from a thousand lifetimes sifted through the tunnel of consciousness and then evaporated back into the universe of potential. Nikki was smiling from ear to ear, because it had been a long, hard journey to get to the edge of humankind, but it had been worth it. As she sought more of the tribe's frantic control and demented discretion, she never felt so complete in all her life.

Her friends were delighted but a bit unnerved by the architects of dance in front of them. The medicine men became more and more possessed in their actions, virtually transforming into their animal counterparts. Garo was deep into their session, bobbing to the beat of boa-skinned drums, while Charge had closed his eyes and was listening to the insight of his buzz.

Billy was satisfied with what he saw, but could never go far enough in to appreciate the real message in the vibrant movements. As far as he was concerned their display was not a life-altering passage into the unknown, it was simply good entertainment. Still, as fun as it all was, as much as the events reminded him of their wildest parties, their craziest nights, he was clear that this was no act. The shamans sensed his complacency, his smugness, and his anxiety. When their violent gestures, bulging eyes, and guttural grunts exploded inches away from Billy's face, he lurched back in fear.

And if he cared about himself a little bit more, he might have even been afraid for his life. Instead, he just sat there, dumbfounded by their maddening domination.

Attempting to save face, he finally turned to Charge and said with a touch of his dry humor, "What the hell is this, a pack of monkeys?"

There was laughter, but he was right, it truly was a monkey dance. The wiry, brooding men had given up human consciousness to become animals incarnate, having reached the coveted point of entrance with their universal ancestors. They were leaping and jumping on all fours, honoring past kills and posing for future abundance. Genuinely wild, they couldn't seem to leave Billy alone. Through their heightened instincts and primordial traits, they sensed a disturbance in the pecking order, and let him know it.

On the other side of the uma, everything was going splendidly for Nikki. She was gaining more than she could have ever imagined from the cultural blast. The hard drugs and magical potions had allowed her to fully connect with the Mentawai state of arousal. When she entered their collective trance, the untamed forces arrived. The smoke swirled in slow motion and Nikki began to make out startling images of clutching paws and biting fangs. She perceived the ancestors, both animal and man, as they entered the room to interact with the world of flesh.

Astonished by the decomposition of her rationality and the zenith of her senses, Nikki grabbed Nathan around the waste and began to point to the empty air. He wasn't all the way there with her, but he understood; he felt the source energy all around him.

Nathan's presence was comforting to her, the touch of his skin soothing, because Nikki was seeing, hearing, and feeling much more than she could handle alone. The two of them sat together in-between worlds, listening to endless chants, an eternal song that the shamans would murmur well into the night. When the rhythms drove the billowing smoke to settle in front of her, she saw the outline of a lean face open its mouth to howl, and she fully comprehended the buried language of animism.

It was then when Charge pointed through his blurred smile and said, "Look, the monkey men are talking to the monkey ghosts."

But Billy, shining with glee from too much hash, was done with the whole affair. Growing restless and insecure from the threat of assault, he needed to exert his control over the situation, and the only way he knew how to do that was by fucking around. So he stood up and began mocking the men, imitating their movements with comical gestures of his own. He grabbed a few leaves off the floor and put them behind his ears, then jumped up and swung from the sacred archway lined with skulls. Charge couldn't help breaking up with laughter, but the Mentawai, cut off from their spiritual source, were not amused.

The performers were mortified by Billy's obnoxious antics, but chose to ignore him to keep up the tempo. However, when he persisted in doing summersaults across the middle of the floor, they had no other choice than to stop him. One of the young shamans cornered him while still possessed by his animism spirit. The others pinned him against the wall while Billy laughed without restraint.

Nathan was terrified, for he knew things were falling apart, and anticipated the most terrible kind of trouble. Worse, he was coming to the realization that his friend was nothing more than a mindless prick, just like the bastards he'd escaped from in the real world. He was determined not to let things get out of control so he stepped in to steer Billy out of the uma. Of course it was too late, the time for understanding was over, the Mentawai could not deal with the bad karma that Billy had generated. As Nathan tried as diplomatically as possible to pull the shamans off of his dreadful friend, warriors were gathering outside with sharpened knives and festooned spears.

Nathan could barely react when the lot of them rushed in and took him down. In an instant, his only reality was their stinking breath and sharpened teeth, their brownish spittle dripping from filed incisors like snake venom at point blank range. His face was smashed against the dirty floor, but his throbbing eyes were open just enough to see the ghastly faces that hissed at him like feral cats. He saw the snarling hatred, their prehistoric contempt for the civilized world, and he felt sorry for them. On some level, he was ashamed to be human.

When he could struggle no longer and was thoroughly pinned to the ground, he began to endure jagged points denting his skin, tearing into his flesh. But the pain came to a halt when a deafening blast shook the dry leaves clear through the roof. The natives stiffened and drew back their grip. Nathan was able to glance over his shoulder and saw Billy wielding a gun over his head, that cocky smile filling in his thoughts. He pointed his ultimate connection

185

with spirit at each of the crazed men and asked if any of them wanted to eat a bullet and visit their ancestors early. Billy had taken back his control.

Unfortunately, the bizarre situation was still salvageable in Charge's mind. He stumbled to the center of the hot zone, grabbed Billy's arm, and shoved the gun to his side. Chasing his own warped sense of culture and tradition, he wanted to smooth things over so he could get back to partying with the primates. It was clear that he'd planned this moment many times in his mind as he held up his hands to make the peace. "All right, all right," he began, "come on all of ya's. Settle down."

Having grabbed their attention, he pulled up a low table, climbed on top, and stood on its sturdy center. He poured a tall glass of hard rum, grabbed a torch from the wall and lit the flammable liquor. With all eyes on him, he raised his blazing cup to the tribesman and said, "Listen, all of you. These guys have put on a hell'uv'a show for us and I'd like to repay you all with something that's dear to my heart. I want to make a toast to all of us. So instead of fighting, let's get drunk together with something I like to call firewater."

It was a monster of a flaming shot, as the boiling cocktail leapt out of its container like an active volcano. Some of the Mentawai elders smiled at Charge's candor while others looked at him with confused grimaces. Billy sighed and started to put his gun in his belt while Nikki took a breath for the first time in minutes.

But just as Charge held his peace offering to his lips, the smallest warrior charged forward and shoved the table out from under him. Charge came down with a thud and looked up to see that his hand was on fire. In the split second that followed, he could only laugh, which allowed many others to join him. But as the blistering alcohol ran down his arm and poured with lava-like ferocity on his face, neck, and chest, the situation turned critical. The big man threw down the cup but the concoction splashed with white-hot passion all over his body. Liquid flames cut through his shaggy chest, dripped onto his inner thighs, and rolled into the creases of his tender crotch. Writhing in pain and screaming with agony, he spun around on the dry floor, begging anyone and everyone to help him. For nearly five seconds, no one could move as they watched the rising inferno in the center of the sacred uma. Nathan finally grabbed a hanging arrangement of woven leaves from the ceiling and leapt on Charge with all he had.

Billy was cool under pressure and understood the consequences of the action before the next step had become clear. He aimed his gun across the room and fired at the lower section of the young Mentawai who had shoved Charge from his stage. When the teenage boy pulled back his foot, a splatter of thick red tissue and bone was left trembling next to a dark hole in the floorboard. The teenage boy went down to the ground and pressed some alalapet leaves against his missing toes, but refused to show any sign of pain.

There were screams, grunts, crackling wood, and the smell of burnt flesh while Nathan hurried to extinguish Charge's searing wounds. The catastrophic climax was upon them. Spirit-filled flames were climbing the dried vegetation and eating the paper-thin walls while the Mentawai warriors fought through the fire in attempt to rout their adversaries.

Mass confusion ensued and Nathan saw countless feet, arms, and spearheads approaching him through the smoke. He wouldn't let Charge die alone, so he made the commitment to stay and fight. But Garo appeared out of nowhere, dragged Nathan and Charge to their feet, and jumped straight through the wall to escape the firestorm in front of a volley of spears. Poisoned tips ripped into the thatched covering on the outside, but they had missed their mark. Nathan and Garo managed to lug their stumbling friend into the thick cover of night.

On the other side of the uma, Billy tore a torch off the wall and made a desperate rush, blasting right over two armed teens at the entrance. Seconds later, he was running alone in the black forest.

## 15.

A steady rain was drumming the dark canopy of leaves as Nathan and Garo followed slick log trails by touch into the pitch of night. Their progress was slow and dismal because Charge had lost consciousness and they were forced to carry him on their shoulders or drag him through the mud. As they wove in and out of the narrow paths and thick cover, a barrage of hushed, menacing voices compelled them to pick up their pace. Uncertain where they were going or how they could escape, they ran recklessly into the black void and grew utterly lost. But minutes later, Nathan stumbled upon the riverbank when he plunged headfirst down the steep embankment while scouting ahead. He and Garo pulled Charge down the bank and waited for the others along the edge of the murmuring water.

The immediate end was to comfort their shredded companion. Charge had always symbolized ruggedness and toughness within the group, but he was in terrible shape and getting worse. His numbing high had worn off and he writhed in agony whenever he came to. He had only his stubborn willpower to deal with the open blisters that were shouting at the stinging air with deformed mouths and his charred shorts that were peeling away blackened skin from his thighs like a grater. Unable to stand Charge's suffering another second, Nathan got out a bottle of aspirin from his pack and forced his friend to swallow six or seven tablets. But they did little to alleviate the pain. His nerve endings were still on fire, causing excruciating curses to resonate above the tree line. They were in danger of being discovered and something had to be done until they could get him medical attention. So Nathan decided to burry Charge up to the neck in the cool mud, hoping the thick moister would act as a sort of ointment.

The mineral bed gave Charge some respite and he crashed into a troubled sleep. While Nathan and Garo stared into the shadowed kingdom for answers, an orange torch appeared in the darkness, bobbing up and down along their sightline as if held by an imperceptible ghost. The guys sat motionless with apprehension until they recognized Billy's hushed voice calling for them. When he appeared at the top of the bank, he quickly cracked a joke about their action-packed escape, but Nathan couldn't pretend to enjoy the situation. Sick with disdain and uncertainty, he asked, "Where's Nikki?"

"I thought you guys pulled her out."

"No, we didn't have time…Holy shit, she's gone."

Billy's easy demeanor turned to sudden rage. "God damn it, what the fuck's wrong with those people. Stay here, I'm going back for her."

Nathan began to climb the bank. "I'm going with you."

"Stay. I'll do it myself. Easier to sneak around alone, and if they see me I'll seem less threatening." He looked down at his buddy and winced when he saw his mud-caked, flaming cheeks. "You stay here, Charge needs you. I'll find her, I promise"

Before Nathan could muster a protest, Billy tossed the torch down the bank and was gone. Once again, Nathan found himself praying to God, begging the universe for Nikki's safe return. He tried to hide his tears from Garo, but saw that his usually laidback friend was just as shaken.

Eventually, Nathan plunged into a nightmare-infested sleep, watching himself chase Nikki's freshly tattooed, bloated body as it perpetually floated just ahead of him in the current. Frantically trying to force himself out of the dream, he could not break the dark grip of his subconscious and kept right on following her. At last, he was startled awake by an echoing blast that shattered the silence of the night. Nathan opened his eyes, waiting for the pointed ends of spears to fill his vision, but realized they were still alone.

Dawn was approaching and they needed to head upstream if they were going to avoid a morning capture. He shook Garo awake and asked what they were going to do about Charge. They hoped the mud had formed a barrier to block the harsh truth, but what they found when they uncovered him was more revolting than the burns. Charge's wounds had become infested with a host of larva and worms gorging on his secreting fluids. Although the crawlers might have ultimately helped with his infection, the guys pulled him into the river and washed away the maggoty creatures with reckless haste.

It was during this bath that Billy appeared again at the top of the bank, just before first light. Nathan at once realized that he had returned empty handed, yet another broken promise. When the run-down leader slid down the hill to offer a hand, Nathan grabbed him by the shirt and demanded, "Where is she?"

Billy tried to play it cool. "I don't know, man. I went to that burned-out hut, peaked around all over, but she was nowhere. I did all I could but a few of the natives spotted me so I had to get out of there in a hurry. We need to keep moving, those fuckers are still on my ass. Trust me, she'll turn up soon."

Garo looked into his eyes and asked, "Are you telling me you're prepared to leave without her?"

"No, but we can't do anything right now, or we'll be dead before morning. What we need to do is get back to Padang and get the authorities involved."

Billy turned and began tramping through the shallows along the edge of the river. Nathan was torn to pieces, but had no other choice but to move on. The three of them cupped Charge in their arms and guided him above the quivering surface of the water, desperate for sanctuary. As Nathan slogged along, he imagined that Nikki was hiding on the banks of the river, that they'd see her around the next turn. But she was never there, only endless foliage and cover.

Billy tried to talk them into a plan to get back safely, but Garo just nodded to the wind while Nathan couldn't bring himself to look up from Charge's conquered expression. Destructive thoughts filled his mind. He understood that if you gamble often enough, if you roll the dice with life's precious balance time after time, then one day you'll get burned. He knew something horrible had happened to Nikki and hated himself for it. And then there was the gang. As far as he was concerned, they were a bunch of selfish idiots who were doing nothing for the world except asking for trouble. But most disheartening were the old thoughts that were resurfacing; Nathan began to fixate on the idea that things would be much easier if he could just take his own life.

About a mile upstream they waded up to their first break in days. An abandoned canoe tied to some overhanging trees was waiting for them in the tranquil undercurrent as a gift from the heavens. They hauled Charge up into it and laid him in the curved interior. Then they took turns paddling while one of them stayed in the water to help pull the overcrowded vessel upstream. It was slow going, but they worked together to create an effective system of progress.

And after nearly two days of continuous struggle, they spotted the final leg on their route back to the Zodiac. Yet, as the trailhead came into view, they saw a Mentawai canoe beached on the sandbar and two silhouettes hiding in the nearby scrub bush beside the waterway. Billy and Garo hopped in the water and hid with Nathan behind the cover of their canoe as they pushed it towards the shore.

Billy pulled out his pistol and peaked around the corner to get a look at the jungle dwellers. Confirming that they were indeed watching him, he took a deep breath and aimed his site at the concealed figures. Then, in his most intimidating voice, he shouted, "Who goes there!" He clutched the trigger and saw dark hair and feminine features winding through the branches. Relieved, he waved and made out Nikki's striking eyes gazing cautiously from the undergrowth.

It was Suku that had saved her. The Mentawai girl had given up her new status with her family to make sure Nikki had been properly taken care of her. Although a cultural outcast, she seemed to be the only one with a sense of humanity left in her.

Nathan nearly fell backwards into the water as he breathed the biggest sigh in his life. He stormed the shore with the intention of giving Nikki an enormous hug, but she wouldn't have it. Instead, she slapped him across the face and said, "Step back, you bloody chook."

She refused to speak to any of the others, but showed great concern for Charge, gently stroking his forehead while repeating words of comfort and encouragement to her large friend. Nikki was devastated by the degradation of the experience and blamed all of them for Charge's injuries. In order to drive her point home, she jogged up ahead, forcing the guys to speed up and make excellent time while hauling Charge through the deep thickets and snaking trails.

It was a long, quiet hike back to the beach. There was an air of a lost battle, a sense of desperate retreat into the depths of shame and guilt. The guys were able to keep busy in their efforts to ease Charge's pain, but they grew more troubled when he didn't stir for hours. Nathan tried several times to break the ice with Nikki, but she resisted, choosing to remain isolated in Suku's company.

At last, they broke out of the maddening wasteland and caught a glimpse of the regal *Rumrunner* from the shimmering beach, which granted them a renewed hope. Nikki said her goodbyes to her extraordinary friend and then jumped onto the Zodiac, isolating herself in the front of the raft. The guys propped Charge up by the engine, waved to the lone heroine standing on the shoreline, and were off.

Upon reaching its sleek bow, the vessel never felt so much like home. They relinquished responsibility of Charge to Kerby and the crew, and then went their own ways to empty cabins. The gang had been awake for days on end, and each of them fell into a cavernous sleep. For a time, there were no negative thoughts, strained emotions, or damaged affections as they recuperated their lost energy and depleted resolve.

When Nikki awoke late the next evening, a leaden despair followed her back to the world of consciousness. She moved about warily, but there wasn't a soul stirring on the decks or in the halls of the drafty ship. Her unsolicited foresight was answered when she went down to check on Charge and discovered that he was gone.

She stormed into Billy's cabin, banged the walls, and poured a pot of icy water over his head.

While trying to remember where he was, Billy shouted, "What the hell's going on? Can you calm yourself down?"

Nikki was furious as she smacked him upside the head and demanded, "What the hell did 'ye do with him, huh? Tell me wha' ye did with Charge?"

In the middle of his soaked recollection, Billy remembered his decision from the previous day. He said in his soothing voice, "Listen, I dropped Charge off in Padang so he could get some treatment. I didn't think we could wait to get to Bali and Garo volunteered to go with him so we just did it."

Nikki was almost growling, her accent intensified by her anger, when she asked, "Whoy didn't you let me off the bloody ship with them, huh Billy? Whoy can't you let me out of yo'r noightmare?"

Billy's patience was spent as he pulled a wet pillow over his head. "Relax you freak. I didn't want to bother you, that's all. It was hectic and Charge was moaning for help so Garo said he'd help him find a hospital. So I gave him some money and they left. I didn't give it another thought. I thought you'd be happy that we did the right thing."

She was crying as she shouted, "Listen you prick, take me back to that city roight now!"

"Hey I don't know what I did to you, but-"

"I said I want to go back roight bloody now, I'm done on this ship."

"Nikki, I can't do that now, things have come up. But I'll get you back as soon as I can." When she raised her hand to slap him again, he turned it up a notch. "Now you settle yourself down and get out of my room, before I throw your ass off this ship."

"Is that a threat, you dog?" Wild with fury, she slammed the decorative door with all her might, causing the doorframe to rip away from the wall. But she hadn't done enough so she opened the door and slammed it six or seven more times until it was merely hanging from its hinges. A few crewmembers had begun to gather in the hall. Nikki started for her cabin, but turned around and appeared in his doorway one more time. She pointed at him and shouted, "You're responsible for all this, all of it!" Bearing a wicked scowl, she concluded, "What you're doing to me is worse than kidnapping."


16.


Nathan heard the commotion and stumbled out to the main deck to try and calm Nikki. She was inconsolable, weeping without shame, striking walls without pain. He apologized four or five times, but she wouldn't even look at him. He'd had it with the way she was treating him so he grabbed her by the shoulders, shook her back into the moment, and said, "Enough of this, you need to talk to me."

Having no one else to turn to, she buried her fists into his chest and then held him with all her might. At length, she confided, "All I want to do is go home."

"You will. We just need to make it through the next few weeks until we can get off this ship."

She turned on him. "You don't understand; it doesn't matter if I get off. I'm not worried about my bloody life."

"Then what is it?"

"Don't you know by now you fool?" She tried to put into words the inexpressible void of her churning emotion. "I came on this trip to learn something about myself, do something more for mankind. But all I've found is that there are no mysteries worth revealing and the only secret is how utterly selfish we all are. No one cares. No one bloody cares about all that's happening in this world."

Billy had come up from below deck in time to catch her last comments. He only wanted things to get back to their simple beginnings. But Nikki was in the midst of a major breakdown, the beginning of a personal transformation that would bring her lifetimes of strength and dignity. When he moved towards her, she retreated to the edge of the bar, grabbed a full bottle of whiskey from behind the counter, and threatened to launch it at him.

Billy truly couldn't understand what he'd done wrong. He begged, "Nikki, I feel horrible about Charge, but I don't know what to do. Please, tell me how to make this better."

She shot back, "Gimme off your buggerin' ship!"

"I told you, you need to be patient. I'm doing all I can."

His empty words stirred her fury and she swung the bottle at a glass dolphin mounted on the back mirror. The sculpture shattered and sweet brown liquor splattered on Billy's chest and waist. Nikki screamed, "Did you hear me, I want to get off roight now!"

Billy was devastated by his inability to smooth things over. "Nikki, why do you hate me? I've given you the time of your life. All I wanted was for all of us to have fun. Is that really so wrong?"

"You honestly have no remorse, do you?"

His grief was turning to anger. "I have no remorse? Do you think I'm not sorry for what's happened?" Billy's grand design had broken down and he was suffering a different kind of collapse, one that would forever rob him of his carefree lifestyle. He did his best to empty his heart out to her. "Do you have any idea what happened when I went back to that fucked-up village to search for you? No? Then let me tell you how small-minded I am, my lady. See, I was alone in the undergrowth near that madhouse and I thought I heard your voice behind me in the trees. So I turned around and took a few steps towards the darkness and saw one of those crazy bastards flying at me from the treetops. And before I could even think about it, I pulled out my gun and fired." Tears welled in his eyes as he cornered Nikki near the back railing. "Don't you understand, I shot one of those little monkeys, God damn it. I fucking killed him too; I know because I saw the death in his eyes. And I did it for you Nikki; I did it because I was trying to rescue you. So don't tell me I don't fucking care."

Nikki was hardly impressed by his confession. In fact, she grew even more revolted by their level of miscommunication. Without another thought, she climbed to the top of the railing and leaned her body into the breeze. "Wha'd ya think now hero? I can jump over if I choose and Charge won't be here to save me. And when I'm gone, after you drink away your false pain, you'll be back at it again, getting on with your game. Because even though you think so, you don't care what you do to people."

Billy just wanted to do what he did best, which was make peace. "Come on Nikki, get down, I don't want this to get worse."

"What're you gonna do, shoot me?" Nikki laughed without humor. "You have you're stories and adventures to brag on, but when you wake up in the middle of the night in a cold sweat, you know exactly what you are."

Billy gave her a look like she was the only one on earth who'd figured him out. He advanced, grabbed her around the waist and pulled her back onto the deck. He glanced back at Nathan as he pinned her to the ground and spoke. "Listen to me. I need you to know some things. First of all, I know everything is falling apart and I'm as fucked up as they come. I know there's nothing else to say to change it but I'm willing to do anything to get things going again in the right direction."

Nikki interrupted, "Oh yah mate, are you ready to go back there and take care of your friend?"

"Listen, I'm planning to pick up Charge and Garo as soon as I take care of a few things. I may have made some mistakes, but you can't accuse me of being an unfaithful friend."

"You don't know what faithful is."

Billy realized he couldn't win her back or even plant the seed of compromise. He'd lost Nikki forever and there was no reason to hold onto his secret any longer. "You're talking about being

199

faithful? That's funny!" He squeezed her firmly and spoke into her distant eyes. "I might not know much, but I know one thing. I know that the two of you have been fucking for months. I know I gave the two of you everything and you went and fucked around right under my nose."

Nikki turned to Nathan for support, but he could only look on at their showdown with a blank stare, unable to move toward them or walk away, wondering if he should fight or apologize. Billy continued, "What am I supposed do about it, huh Nikki? Do you think I didn't want to kill that prick over there because he's giving you what you need? I wish I could, but no, there's nothing I can do except live with the two of you fuckin' like bunnies in *my* bed, aboard *my* ship. And do you know why? Huh? It's because I love you, that's why. I love you both and need you in my life."

Nikki, refusing to give in to his emotional plea, looked up at his twisted face and tried to wiggle from his grasp. As she cranked her head and neck away from his revolting lips, she murmured, "Did you ever consider the fact that I don't need you?"

It was then that Nathan witnessed the all-in gamble from his desperate friend. Billy released Nikki, pulled her to her feet, and got back down on his knees. From there, he pleaded, "Come on Nikki, it's not supposed to end like this. Listen, I'll take you to Fiji, that's where you've always wanted to go, isn't it? We'll get one of those bungalows on a lagoon and get our minds together. If you take some time to think things through and nothing changes, then that's it. I'll understand."

200

Nikki seethed, "I don't want anything more to do with you." She saw her chance, lunged forward, and struck Billy in the groin, and he was forced to wrestle her back to the hard deck.

Despite his guilt-ridden melancholy, Nathan found the nerve to jump on the ex-lovers in attempt to wrench them apart. As he pried the hands of his best friend off of his girl, he regained his voice. "Billy, let go of her before I beat your head in. It's too late for apologies, we just need to move on."

The guys got to their feet and began to brawl, slamming each other into a wall and then back down to the wooden floor. Nikki stepped past them and disappeared downstairs, and the guys quickly realized they were fighting over a girl who wanted nothing to do with either of them. They let go of each other, turned onto their backs, and let out panting breaths, all the while looking up from their tiny stage at the captivated stars. The surge of madness passed. Minutes later, they were shamefully drinking together at the bar, aware that the good times might be behind them, but content to shoot the shit about the endless memories they shared.

Yet, when late morning rolled around and the guys woke to their pathetic realities, reminiscent stories could no longer bring them together. The silence on the ship made it all too clear. Times of boom are inevitably followed by times of bust. The perfect wave perpetually crashes against jagged rocks. For Billy and Nathan, the merciless consequences of life had tracked them for too many months and had finally caught up with them, forcing them to pay their dues.

Despite Billy's incoherent ramblings about another new adventure, Nathan felt like a captive within his own freedom. He knew death was only one bad decision away so he went back to the crow's nest to ponder his miserable choices and plan an escape. There was no one to talk to about his concerns, but he'd climb down from his upper circle three times a day to leave plates of food outside Nikki's door. Upon returning, he'd sometimes find an empty tray or a brief note, but more often the cold food remained sitting where he'd left it.

With Billy's forced exodus of the rest of the guests and most of the crew in Padang, the ship had become a virtual ghost-liner. Once again, the reflective sea brought Nathan nothing but further isolation and loneliness. There was no more music. There was no more fun. There was no more hope. Time dragged like a mind-numbing lecture as the vast horizon seemed to cause every moment to pause and stand still before moving on into the breeze.

And the more Billy began to secretively plot with Kerby on the bridge, the more Nathan wondered just how irrational and dangerous his friend had become. When he sat alone and allowed the tides into his thoughts, the deep told him that there were no more answers because he had ceased to ask the right questions. A part of him had become afraid for his life, convinced that Billy was seeking revenge for their affair. And as he grew more intolerant of their unknown destination, he decided to climb to the captain's quarters to confront Billy.

Upon reaching the bridge, Nathan realized that Billy had lifted the restrictions on Kerby's old habits. The two of them were sitting on the floor with black residue spread about their hands and thighs and a funky pipe resting on Kerby's lap. Nathan suddenly understood why the ship was looping listlessly toward the starboard side. He straightened out the wheel and insisted that Kerby go downstairs to give him some time alone with Billy.

Nathan sat down beside his buddy and sighed, then shook his head in disgust. After some time, he asked, "Billy, how you doing?"

"Neva' felt better, my brotha."

Despite his contempt and suspicions, Nathan tried to sound sincere. "I can't tell you how sorry I am for what's happened between Nikki and me. I swear I didn't mean to keep it from you, but I love her."

Billy, strung out beyond comprehension, took another hit from the ivory pipe and squinted in his friend's direction. He'd aged ten years in the past few days due to the constant highs and lows that were finally taking their toll. After a long pause he said, "Don't lose anymore sleep o'er it my friend, it's not what you think." His words were running together as he continued, "Ya'know, Nathan, I sometimes wonder if I'm not a faggot or somethin', because I sum'times think'ov ya making love to her right under my nose, on my ship, in my bed, and it makes me sort'a happy."

"I don't want to hear-"

"It's almost as if I wish I could watch the two of you, or be one of you, because you got something that I can never have. That's the real reason why I can't let you go, because the two of you together seem to keep my motor runnin'."

The bizarre statement caused Nathan to lose his patience. "Listen, I don't know what you're talking about, but I'm here because it's time you let us off the ship. Billy, Nikki said she didn't want to go to Fiji with you, so where the hell are you taking us?"

Billy flashed a vacant smile and asked, "You don't get it, do you?"

"Get what?"

The hollow man was incapable of giving a straight answer but his voice was steady, calm. "Well, our next adventure will be a little more real, 'cause my life is smack dab in the sights of obliteration. See, when I gave Garo that cash to take care of Charge, I realized no one's been keeping track a'my shit like they should. I finally figured out that most of my money's been wasted or stolen and I don't have much left other than this boat. So this is it, the last hurrah brotha'. And before I give it up, there are a few more places I need to go." He put his arms around Nathan and blubbered, "But I promise, after our next stop, we're on our way to Fiji."

Nathan tried to interrupt, "I told you she-"

But Billy just kept right on talking, "We'll get Nikki to those islands this time, I promise. And I'll have a new roll of cash when my investments come in, an' then we can get clean and start all over again." As he fumbled to get a needle from his small duffle, he mumbled a few more inaudible promises into the dark. After tying a rubber hose firmly around his bicep, his hands shook to load the modern crucifix from his blackened spoon, but he didn't spill a bead of the silvery liquid. And as he injected the devil's juice into his faded spirit, Nathan watched him slip into the blissful realm of living

204

ghost. Lifetimes of inspiration and wisdom poured through his thoughts, although they would never make it out to the breathing side of consciousness.

There was nothing for Nathan to do except walk away. He climbed to the top of his tower, curled up into a pathetic ball, and cried. After glimpsing the extent to which Billy had fallen, he resolved to sneak Nikki off at the next port, whatever the consequences.

A few days later, he got a dreadful dose of reality when he discovered their destination looming on the edge of the world. In front of him was the outline of the volatile nation of Papua-New Guinea, one of the most beautiful and dangerous places on earth. He climbed down from his post to enquire about the motivation for their odd objective. Billy played the role of reckless fool to perfection, heightening Nathan's anxiety with descriptions of the country's cultural isolationism and regressing tribal warfare. He told exaggerated stories of hundreds of clans that spoke over a thousand languages and fought over the same hills for generations, and concluded that the turbulent locals had a reputation for annihilating unwanted guests. Nathan knew there was more than a sliver of truth to what Billy was saying, so when he weighed his options, he determined that there was absolutely no way he'd take his chances by escaping to those deadly shores. Uneasy patience would have to persist.

Cruising the threatening coast from a safe distance was one thing, but Nathan couldn't imagine what possessed Billy to head to land the next morning. But when he started bragging about Kerby's revered knowledge of a great treasure amidst the depths of a clannish war, their motivation became crystal clear although their strategy left something to be desired. Billy asked Nathan to take part in their mission, but he flat out refused.

Kerby was all that Billy had left to play with in his wicked little game. Although he had won the struggle against his dark half in recent years, he just couldn't pass up the wild opportunity when Billy came to him from that place of cold desperation. There was a fresh sparkle in Kerby's eye, an impression of self-importance in his actions, as he made the necessary preparations for their covert operation. He was reinvigorated, as after all, he'd been chosen as Billy's first lieutenant, his new main man. And with his deep sense of island wisdom and cultural savvy, he might have even called himself *Tuan Kerby* because astonishing stories from his youth fostered a legendary status.

Of course, the easy confidence he portrayed before entering hostile territory had rubbed off on the vacant depths of Billy's character. The creepy pleasure in Billy's voice, mocking the gods of mortality, spoke of his excitement for living a heartbeat ahead of death. While preparing to shove off, he raised his eyebrows at Nathan and taunted, "You still planning on making a run for it partner?" Then, while laughing from the Zodiac, he shouted, "I disabled the radio, but, if you wanna' go for a tour in the other inflatable, be my guest."

Nathan did his best to ignore the challenge, focusing on his crumbling relationship with Nikki. When the two men were gone, he tapped on her door for more than half an hour. He talked through the wood barrier, explaining Billy's state of mind and their possible options. But she would have none of it. He heard her challenge him with cutting words. "You watch me stand up to him and do nothing. You think you love me but allow us to stay on this ship. What kind of a man are you?"

He was hurt by her challenge, but held it in and tried to remind her why they were together. He spoke about their favorite memories together, laughing to himself about their intimate sea excursions. She could no longer hide from the fact that she loved him despite his faults. Soon a smile was beaming through her tears and she wavered and opened the door. A twinge of regret dropped through Nathan's heart when he saw how delicate and vulnerable she appeared, while her unkempt demeanor revealed her glowing natural beauty. Currents of energy rippled through his skin as he took her in his arms and rediscovered the joy of human contact. They lay together in her bed for the rest of the afternoon, catching up on weeks of lost intimacy.

Billy and Kerby emerged from their secret rendezvous three days later, compelling Nikki back to her hideaway. The men were in high spirits, boasting about the apparent success of their mission despite having returned empty-handed. And after a few shots at the bar, they made their way to the bridge to change the ship's course. They were meticulous in comparing scribbled notes to their detailed charts, finally heading towards a group of ragged islands off the east coast.

A few hours later, Billy hooted with excitement when he saw the remains of a beached ship that had been ripped in two, rising out of the water like an iron land mass. When the charts confirmed the discovery of their gold mine, he put his arm around Nathan and said, "Come with us buddy, this is one of the most unique spots you'll ever surf."

Nathan thought Billy had literally lost his mind when he realized that their coveted treasure was nothing more than directions to an unknown surf spot. He had to laugh as he asked, "Is this really what we're here for you stupid bastard?" Yet, he found appreciation in Billy's undying hunger for that youthful shine. Despite the fact that every aspect of his life had collapsed under him, the man only wanted to have a few more moments of uninterrupted fun. So with nothing to lose but his own self-respect, Nathan decided to humor his friend and surf with him one last time.

Billy was able to navigate the *Rumrunner* through the deep water near sheer cliffs so they could anchor relatively close to the beached wreck. Once moored, they stared from the rail at their first full view of the extraordinary waves. About a hundred yards from shore, the manmade break daunted them, as curling tubes ran through the invisible center of the ship and then crashed against its tangled stern.

Kerby appeared from below deck with an armful of glistening boards. Surprisingly, he carried a massive long board of his own, a masterpiece of craftsmanship decorated with radiant tropical scenes from around the world. He pointed up to Billy on the bridge and asked, "Are you ready to find your dream?" Then, for the first time since joining the crew, the wind-worn master of adventure tossed his board over the rail and dove into the water.

Billy and Nathan followed him in and soon they were on their way in for a closer look at the wreck. While they paddled towards the jagged sections of the liner, Billy explained that it had been a Japanese merchant ship that was torpedoed at the end of the Second World War. Upon drifting up to its disintegrating mass, Nathan was impressed with the artistry of the saw-toothed metal simultaneously exposing the exterior surface and interior frame of the hull. Its burnt-orange skin was decaying like a dead body, forcing Nathan to think about all those who must have lost their lives in the attack.

An odd sense of deja vu overcame him; triggering a feeling not that he'd been there before, but that he would be there again. This pulsating apprehension allowed Nathan to take it all in and focus on every weather-beaten detail. As he passed a row of seabirds lining a rusted cable, they scattered like a squadron of squawking warplanes, leaving the lonely wire dangling in the crystal clear waters. Nathan drifted under the corroded anchor resting half way up the hull and could almost make out the outline of a series of Japanese symbols printed above the old waterline. He felt like a child in the midst of a massive war game when he paddled by the heat-bowed tower and bomb-damaged bridge. And when he glanced back at the face of the arched bow thrusting out of the water like a rusty iceberg, the sheer size of the wreck made him feel small and uneasy. More than anything, he wanted to climb aboard and open his thoughts to this gateway through history.

He figured Kerby had the same juvenile idea when he spotted the grizzled man climbing the short distance up the side of the hull. Nathan made his way back to the bow and followed him up to the sheered edge where the ship was split in two. From there, they clambered up the deck in an almost vertical assent until they reached the tip of the liner sticking high in the air. With feet wedged in a gaping crack and hands gripping the rusty rail, they looked down on the palm-lined shoreline with pleasure. Kerby spotted jagged machine gun holes lining the face of the deck and reached to put his finger through one, and then pointed to the dual gun turrets mounted on the stern across the waterway.

Nathan shook his head at the symbolic implications of the view and said, "Crazy shit, to be a part of all this. But it sure is beautiful up here."

Kerby scoped the distant skyline for signs of trouble and asked, "You really don't know why I'm up here, do you?"

"What do you mean?"

"Oh, nothing." He smirked, "You just keep letting that shine of yours blind you. It's better that way." Then, after another quick scan of the ocean, he climbed over the rail, spread his arms to the heavens, and jumped. Nathan watched in perplexed wonder as Kerby tumbled through the air in a summersault and then straightened out into a dive at the surface of the water.

Again, Nathan followed his cruel mentor into the exhilarating unknown. The rush of air took his breath away as he completed a sixty-foot swan dive into the deep turquoise blue, and once more he remembered why he was alive.

Billy had laid the boards on the slanted deck and was waiting for them at the threshold where the water met the wreckage. The three men had to dive eight feet under and squeeze through a serrated opening to reach the dark expanses of the interior. They then followed a soggy map by lighter through crooked corridors and narrow halls, often climbing sideways down ladders until they reached the open expanse of the forward hold. A blanket of darkness engulfed them although shards of sunlight lashed through a thousand geometric holes in the ceiling and walls, enhancing the surreal setting.

Kerby searched rusted compartments and lifeless storerooms with grim curiosity. But after a few minutes of exploration, he seemed satisfied and sat down on an iron platform to have a smoke in the isolation. Billy unwrapped a small pipe from his suit and convinced them to smoke a bowl right there. After a few hits, he had them sucked into one of his infamous stories, this one describing a worn Japanese naval officer he'd met in Saigon who'd lost his ship in the Battle for Guadalcanal. The engrossing words and warm hum in Nathan's mind told him that it was alright to surrender to the splendor one last time. But, after nearly falling into the chasm of spiraling time, Kerby halted the story and said, "Listen, the two of you should go surfing because I have some work to do."

Life was good as they paddled into a break together with clear, jovial minds. The warm water and fascinating setting only intensified Nathan's high, and for the last time ever it felt like old times. Surfing with Billy was no longer a competition, but the final glimpse of liberty. The fun little waves were a challenge because if you caught one just right, you could surf right through the two halves of the ship, peering into the dark interior as you rode by. One time, as Nathan passed by a decayed section of the hull, he thought he saw a shadowy figure peeling back the top of his board.

While relaxing in the sun, Nathan was again lost in Billy's fading sense of paradise. Had he paid more attention to the outside world, he might have noticed the captain repeatedly paddling back and forth from wreckage to the *Rumrunner*. While waiting for the next set to come in, Billy took in the panoramic view and said, "Wow, look at this, it always finds me."

"What's that?"

"Living history. The world wants me to be a part of something larger, something great."

Nathan sighed. "Yes, it does, you're lucky that way. And right now, I'm glad to be a part of it." His allusion towards total collapse had transformed to short-lived respite, luring him into the dreadful web. Maybe his addictions would never allow him to learn life's most important truth.

Billy pressed his illusory dream. "I tell you, I should have fought in a war. I might have lived up to my grandfather's reputation."

Nathan joked back, "I don't know about that." But he saw the desperation in Billy's eyes. "Seriously, you've sure taught me more about history, about life, than any of my teachers. And although this trip's been a crazy roller coaster ride, I'm having fun right now and that's all that matters. One moment at a time, am I right?"

But just as the words left his mouth, he spotted a dark vessel making its way directly towards them. Nathan wanted to ignore the sinking feeling invading the pit of his stomach the same way he'd disregarded the endless list of tragedies that led him to this point. But Billy immediately knew the graveness of their situation and began paddling with all his might towards the *Rumrunner*. Nathan looked around for answers and realized that Kerby was nowhere in sight.

Suddenly feeling utterly alone in his world, he lay motionless on his board and watched the situation unfold as if he were a spectator at an ocean-born coliseum. Unable to move, he gazed at the intimidating gunboat as it raced at him like a vicious water snake. Although it was still some distance off, he could vaguely make out a dark splotch of fifteen to twenty figures readying themselves for attack. And when he felt the first bullet hiss by his head and skip across the smooth ocean surface, Nathan snapped back into the moment and began paddling for his life.

17.

After each stroke Nathan peaked over his shoulder, repeatedly spotting the rebels as they progressed towards him at breakneck speed. The gunboat slowed a few yards behind him, and he could clearly make out the features of the crew. They were clad in dark brown and black uniforms and wore black berets or sun-hats, a frightening cross between navy seals and modern pirates. Their one identifying feature was an intricate patch of a tribal mask on each shirt pocket, keeping traditional culture close to their hearts. One glance at their harsh appearance and it was clear that killing was an everyday part of their existence.

Yet, the menacing unit was only playing with him, pursuing as if they were illicit poachers hunting a wounded marine mammal. Their freakish leader, a tall, emaciated old radical with a huge black head, his apelike face covered in thin lines of war paint, had ordered them to pull alongside the struggling surfer and follow his frantic progress. There were shouts of laughter and Nathan could hear them calling out to him in a pigeon form of Tok Pisin tinged with English, but he just kept right on paddling. When he looked back, he could see their shiny white teeth smiling under black complexions, and could sense their loaded weapons zeroing in on his rear. One time, they moved in so close that Nathan nearly jumped off his board when he felt the muzzle of a machine gun ram into his back. With each shrill cry, he waited for the impact of a bullet in the back, but for some reason they temporarily held their fire.

Then, about a hundred yards from the *Rumrunner*, the sleek vessel gave up its maddening pursuit. Nathan reached the ship's stern just as the giant engines kicked in and began to churn under his feat. He rose from his gurgling board and leapt to the side of the ship, then climbed the wiry ladder with desperate agility. His favorite board was left floating harmlessly in the water. Just for fun, the bandits aimed their AK-47's and opened fire, cutting it to fiberglass shreds.

The coastal raider kept its distance as Nathan tumbled over the rail and dove for cover behind a row of finally carved tables and chairs. From a hundred and twenty yards, the erratic commander picked up a megaphone and began shouting imperceptible threats towards Billy's crew, demanding that they 'halt their engines at once.' Kerby wasn't about to go without a fight and throttled the *Rumrunner* with all her power, compelling the raider to loop around and pull up along her starboard side.

There was a long pause as the invaders waited in their battle positions, and then the 50-caliber mounted machine gun let loose, pelting the hull and main deck with a heavy burst of fire. For a moment Nathan could see the snout of the gun blazing in the distance, but when the blistering mouth turned towards the stern, he was forced to duck behind a marble column and cover his head. The one thought that repeatedly looped through his mind was the fact that these were real bullets gunning for him; this wasn't one of Billy's ridiculous games. The booming cascades rang above him, and he watched in silence as shattered glass, splintered wood, and slashed plants fell in strait lines of ruin.

Hopelessly pinned, he tried to control his shallow sobs and frenzied breathing as ricocheting fragments of sculpture and molding skipped over him. Although the cords of fire just wouldn't let up, he was finally able to get a grip by focusing on a way to get to Nikki before the bandits boarded the ship. The fading ideal of their relationship was the one force that compelled him to take steps to safety. He planned to make a run for it to a concealed section of shrubbery beside the pool, and from there sneak down the stairs to Nikki's room. He began crawling towards the bar but the whole situation became too much to take when he simultaneously felt a hot crackle wiz by his ear and saw a bullet hole appear three inches above his scalp in the thin walls of the bamboo lounge. Right then, he knew he needed to act or die.

But the skipper of the *Rumrunner* didn't waver in his speed or direction, while the    attackers readied their heavy arms. The continuous clatter of the machine gun fire died away and there was a moment of relative calm. Nathan took this chance to make his way towards the sheltered pool area. But as he jogged with his head down, he heard an odd noise that sounded like, "Foooof." There were a few more seconds of silence and then a deafening blast. A mortar shell detonated at the base of the waterfall above the pool, sending synthetic granite, lush ferns, and the base of a hot tub spiraling onto the deck and into the ocean.

The grinning operative of the 81 mm mounted mortar let another round fly. The second shell hit a staircase, shattering the eves holding up the arched balcony on the second deck. A ten-foot long section of the overhang gave way and collapsed onto the bamboo bar.

Seconds later, a third explosion hit the sand area that had been the volleyball court, the force of the impact tossing Nathan through the air. He struck a palm tree in mid air before landing in the pool, and a sharp pain ran down the right side of his back. The world was ringing as he teetered on the verge of shock. While hiding under the surface of the pool, he felt a dull throbbing on his right side and noticed that the water around him had turned a dark pink. Regaining focus over the humming drone inside his head, he realized that a thin eight-inch stake from the volleyball net was sticking out of his shoulder. Fortunately, the metal rod had entered through the back of the shoulder and exited through the top of his triceps. Grabbing the stake with his left hand, he was able to yank it from his skin and toss it in the water. Although a chunk of flesh was hanging from the back of his arm, he was in better shape than some of the others.

After a lull, the gunners picked up movement in various sections of the ship and again sprayed the deck with fire. The smiling rebel gained his bearings and honed in on the greatest weakness of the ship. He launched a mortar shell that exploded in the water at the underside of stern, crippling one of the propellers. Two more shells ripped into the hull at the waterline and the *Rumrunner* began taking on water. From that moment on, the ship would float listlessly in the calm waters, gently spiraling to the starboard side until it met its fate at the bottom of the Solomon Sea.

The gunboat approached in a deliberate fashion, taking time to gauge the damage. Nathan scrambled out of the pool and crawled to the edge of the staircase, where he saw two young women lying motionless in their string bikinis, holding each other in hopeless terror. At first glance, he thought the dark-haired body was that of Nikki, but then felt a raging anguish and relief when he turned her over and got a good look at her lifeless face. It was Gabriel. He held her warm head in his lap, caught a glimpse of Heather's profile, and suddenly understood that both of Billy's most devoted girls were no longer a part of this world.

While fumbling down the stairs with shock waves rippling through his core, he tripped over Billy who'd apparently made it to the stairwell. The man, recklessly liberated from fear, looked up at him and chuckled, "Now, this is a fine mess you've gotten us into. I don't suppose you have any ideas on how we're going to get out of it, do you?"

All Nathan could say was, "Gabe and Heather are dead."

Billy changed his tone, but still sounded thoughtless and carefree. "We're all dead, unless we can save ourselves. Follow me, I know a place that they'll never find us."

"I'm going to get Nikki. You can go do what you want."

"That's fine. But the two of you have no other choice than to follow me. If you want to live that is?"

Up on deck, the corrupt militia had boarded. They were searching the ship for contraband, the hard muzzles of their guns leading the way into every nook and cranny. Spotting the wounded Kerby on the bridge, they pounced on him and tossed him over the railing onto the main deck. Three guards stood over him while the rest of them scoured below deck. Within five minutes, they had rounded up the seven living crewmembers and tossed five dead bodies over board. The battered group was taken to the stern of the ship, pinned to the floor, and with AK-47's pointed in their teeth, forcibly coerced to give up the smuggled goods. The men were humiliated and beaten while the two Indonesian maids were taunted and fondled. By the look in the eyes of rebels, it was clear that they were preparing for a brutal violation.

From his position of submission, Kerby could see the eerie contrast of their tribal paint and pierced noses with their daunting uniforms and intimidating guns. He watched their radical leader pull a thick knife from his belt and tower over him with the blade flashing in the sunlight. The rebel smiled and pointed to the long surfboard that leaned just inside the stairwell. Two of the guards retrieved it and their chief stuck his knife in and cut down the center of the image-covered fiberglass. When he ripped off the nose of the board and dumped out its contents, brick after brick of illegal drugs fell to the ground. The chief had his just cause. He pounded Kerby's head against the ground, mocking in broken English. "Wha' yu tink yu get away wit, eh."

The three survivors peered out from an impeccably hidden hold under the staircase watching the conspiracy unravel. On the other side of the paper-thin wall, they listened to the Papua-New Guinea drug ring dismantle Billy's last desperate attempt at easy money. It was clear the mercenaries would use the confiscated dope for their own profits, proving that Kerby's connections weren't as reliable as he'd thought. Billy aimed his gun out of the crack in the secret door, waiting for someone to spot him, hoping he could end it once and for all. But they didn't come. They routed and looted the burning ship, stripping it of all its valuables, but didn't uncover the storehouse overloaded with cannabis, opium, and heroin.

Nathan, pressed against Nikki in the tight quarters, tried to comfort her the best he could, although he was shaking in his own skin. While anticipating their imminent capture, his mind cleared and the incredible underwater experiences at Midway, the excitement he'd just had on the beached merchant ship, played nostalgically through his mind. He knew that they would soon become a part of that history, another heartbreaking story lost on the ocean floor. Most notably, he felt a touch of irony as he realized with a joyless smile that Billy had finally found his war.

But it was a war he could not fight. Nothing could be done about the miserable struggles occurring on the other side of the wall. Although Billy's luck had run out, he wasn't ready to give it all up just yet. He was perfectly comfortable allowing Kerby to go down for him. Despite two bullet holes in his abdomen and a severely swollen face, Kerby refused to show any signs of weakness to his captors. He remained lively and in high spirits, acting as if he'd been in worse positions in the past. Yet, if someone were to take a closer look at his prematurely aged face, they might have seen the deepening lines around his eyes and forehead. And if they could get inside his mind, they might have heard his uneasy thoughts racing around the impending cruelty. But he was a man's man to the end; an air about him said he'd somehow find a way out. As he was being hauled up the stairs in shackles, he shouted down to the floorboards, "Crazy world isn't it? I'll be back though."

They were the last words his friends ever heard him utter. Billy, Nathan, and Nikki lay silently for quite sometime, wondering if and when it would be safe to come out. But the ship was going down quickly and they were forced to try their luck sooner than they would have liked. After squeezing out of the double blind opening and sneaking up to the main deck, they saw the gunboat just as it was pulling away from the listless ship.

There wasn't any time to think, only react. Amidst the confusion, Billy decided he was going to fulfill his promise to Nikki and head to Fiji, despite other stretches of land that were substantially closer. Billy sent Nathan below deck to get as many gas cans as he could carry so they'd have a chance of completing his final mission. The back deck was under water as Billy opened the bay doors and cranked the lift to access the Zodiac. Nathan returned with four full containers and the guys worked together with terrific efficiency. But while they readied the raft with as much fuel, water, and food as they could scramble together, Nikki was nowhere to be found.

Water poured in past each bulkhead and the ship began to creak deep in her underbelly. Nathan grew dreadfully worried. He raced back and forth from the kitchen expecting to see her around every corner, but quickly lost his patience with each foot of deck space. Finally, his fluttering anxiety compelled him to drop a crate of food and stomp off to the flooded depths of the ship to search for her.

Although in a state of shock, Nikki took her final tour of the ship with a clear-minded grace, searching for meaning that would determine her future despite the desperate circumstances. She had wandered off to her cabin, into Nathan's room, and then to the recording studio, before making her final stop at the small Zodiac on the slanting port side. She packed a small chest with a precious treasure, wrote her parent's address on a sheet of paper, and sealed it so that it was watertight. Nathan finally spotted her struggling to get the boat over the rail and into the water and panicked as he saw her making a go of it alone. Escape was useless without her; if he was going to die, he needed to die in her arms. As he sprinted towards her, preparing to dive in and swim after her until she picked him up or he drowned, he wished they were back at their secluded island together. But by the time he reached her, she had placed the chest in the middle of the small boat, started the engine of the craft, and sent it on its way towards the endless horizon.

He helped her back over the slanted rail and said, "I thought you were leaving me again. What was that all about?"

She replied, "Ask me again someday."

The *Rumrunner* was on the verge of rolling onto its starboard side when they three castaways boarded the overloaded Zodiac and began their fifteen hundred mile journey towards destiny. For nearly twenty minutes, they watched as the bow of the ship increasingly pointed towards the sky. Billy looked back at his grandpa's hopes when the ship grumbled and then capsized, creating a nice size wake that shook them into leaving.

After three days of endless motoring, they used the last drop of gas and came to a deadly rest on the calm sheet of water. But Billy was always prepared and fired flares in the air at hourly intervals. On the fourth day, they were rescued by a chopper a few miles off the coast of Fiji.

18.

Billy lay curled in the king size bed of his over-water bungalow, desperately trying to get his head on straight. Waves of shared misery, self-consumed remorse, and personal responsibility devoured him. The thought of listening to Kerby being dragged away in shackles only substantiated the tremendous guilt that had

222

already deadened his soul. But with the serious consequences of the latest ordeal, he became more open to exploring the motivations of his dark conscience, and might have finally realized just how corrupt his character was.

He didn't want to spend the rest of his days feeling awful. So for the first time in his life, he admitted to himself that the disgrace, degradation, and deaths were at least partly his fault. While measuring his options, a vein of hope began to pulse in his conscience as he considered how liberating it would feel to confess his mistakes to his two remaining friends.

He got up and walked to the window of his royal suite and sighed with sorrowful pleasure at the green cathedral-like spires jutting out from the mountain backdrop. The soft breeze compelled him to step outside onto the stilted deck over the lagoon to thoroughly contemplate his situation. Sitting on a lounge chair soaking in the sun, he realized he would never be the same again. The healing rays brought fresh anticipation to his thoughts, a revival to do everything he had originally set out to do. Nathan's gift for music came to the surface of his mind. Was this the next step on his wild journey? He grinned up at the sky. There was one thing Billy could always rely on; he knew how to reinvent himself.

Yet his growing need for a fix, a mounting dilemma that he couldn't even admit to himself, began to alter his upbeat mood. As he made his way away from the setting sun and back into his isolated room, he longed for that freeing high and dubious interaction. For men like Billy Windsor, loneliness was more difficult to face than any emotion. Sure, he had promised to give Nikki and Nathan their space, but he pictured how much lighter things would be if they would burst in on him right then, hit him in the head with a pillow, pour a stiff drink, and laugh together as if nothing had happened. In fact, he wished he could start the whole trip over again so he could more thoroughly enjoy the days of old.

Just across the lagoon in the other bungalow suite, the troubled couple tried to recover from the intensity of their trauma. Nathan's movement was limited due to the bandages on his arm and shoulder, so they lay together, made some small talk, and slept off the effects of the ordeal. Around four o'clock in the morning, Nathan was startled awake by a deafening dream that escaped his mind as soon as he sat up in bed. He rolled over to find some comfort in Nikki's warm body, but realized she was no longer in bed with him.

He spotted her wistful silhouette on the floor and tried to get her attention, but her head was buried in her arms. She had finally made it to the destination of her dreams, yet the reality didn't at all match her fantasy. Nathan approached her and saw that she was lying partially nude on the glass floor of the hut, a silk sheet falling off her midsection, her circular breasts pressed tightly against the porthole facing to the moonlit sea. Silvery fish flashed swiftly underneath, their thoughtless manner a perfect contrast to her heavy emotion.

The star-filled night was quiet and reflective, allowing them to find a few moments of repose. He sat next to her, never more appreciative to have her in his crumbling world. Something about her countenance and tone told him she needed him as much as he needed her. He massaged her temple, hoping the love they shared could somehow heal all the regret.

Nikki stared down through the built-in aquarium for several minutes. She finally looked to him and asked, "So, what do we do from here, my Luv?"

His answer deflated him before it even left his mouth. "I guess we go home." Then he teased, "Wanna come with me?"

The romanticism of the night had gotten to her and she wouldn't have any dispirited talk. She asked, "Go home? Isn't that like giving up on all your dreams?"

Nathan stared at her shimmering features accented by glowing light from underneath the glass and said, "Not all of them, because I'd still have you. And with all that's happened, I don't think I'll be writing any new songs any time soon. But hey, I've gotta wake up sometime."

Needing to roll the dice of hope one more time, Nikki clung to Nathan's lost ambition. "Come on Luv, I still believe it can all come true for you. You deserve something good to happen. Not to mention, I think I'd be pretty good at helping you along on the road."

The idea of taking a chance together compelled repressed inspiration to the surface. Simple but meaningful lyrics, as uncomplicated as beach sand but as complex as the universe, began to well in his mind. Nikki's desperate aspirations held them together for a few more moments.

But then Nikki's bitterness caused her to take it a step too far. She said, "I have an idea. I'm gonna see to it that Billy invests the rest of his money into you."

"Why would you want to involve him any more?"

"Because the bastard owes us after what he's put us through. He's gotta get some money out'a losing his boat. And if he doesn't want us to talk about all that's happened, he'd be smart to pay us for our pain."

"Nikki, I love you. You have to know how much you mean to me. But listen to me now. I don't want his help. Our lives have fallen apart because of him and I don't care if I see him again."

Irrational thoughts of revenge made her voice sound jovial despite her surging grief. "Who says he needs to be a part of our lives? We take his money, run away together, and create beautiful music."

"I don't think-"

She cupped her hand over his mouth. "I don't bloody care what you think anymore, it's about what you need."

He tried to find her reason. "Nikki?"

"I'll say it one last time. If you don't ask him, I will."

He had no choice but to laugh with her. "Go ahead. There's nothing left he can do to hurt us."

She was talking hurriedly, "You know, I'll hit him where it hurts. Sweet talk him, make him feel like he's important and all that rubbish." She giggled with controlled fury, "And if he doesn't respond, I just might have to kill him."

Dawn's early gleam was lighting the island's higher elevations as Nathan grudgingly agreed to allow Nikki to go over and demand Billy's financial support. With a mind full of loathing, she boarded the resort's kayak and paddled across the bay to his neighboring hut. Along the way, she told herself to be strong, to resist emotion, and to fight back any pity. She would come clean, let out her mixed feelings for him, and find the closure that had been lacking for so long.

Nathan watched her in the distance as she approached the deck; he was nervous about the encounter but delighted to have such a supportive woman on his side. He cringed when Nikki knocked on the door, half expecting to see Billy stumble out the door after another drunken slumber. But he had kept his word and resisted the temptation of drugs or alcohol the previous evening.

When he didn't answer, she peaked in through the open window, and then let herself in. Moments later, Nathan heard the same deafening scream he'd heard in his dream, shattering all thought of a favorable resolution. Knowing Billy had confronted her, he dove in and began swimming towards the other bungalow as fast as he could. As he stroked with all his might, struggling against his wounds, he visualized how hard he was going to hit the man for upsetting Nikki again. He promised that if the scoundrel laid a hand on her, he would knock him right through the paper-thin wall.

By the time he made it to the deck and began to pull himself out of the water, Nikki was standing over him with a sallow expression. Her incoherent words and contorted face kept him in the dark a few more seconds. Then her inflection leveled and he heard her say, "He's dead. He's fucking dead, Nathan. His brains are all over the bamboo walls."

In one motion, Nathan shot out of the lagoon and crashed through the front door. Immediately, he saw the consequences of a deserted life and comprehended how Billy had found his ultimate freedom. The body of the man who'd had so much energy to give was sprawled out backwards on an overturned chair, gun on his chest, the top of his skull scattered in tiny fragments across the back wall. There was no note, but three full glasses of wine sat on the bamboo table. This was Billy's last attempt at remorseful communication, a haunting invitation to join him in his lost world.

Nikki and Nathan stood silent in the entryway, until unrestrained sobs began to escape from her diaphragm. They collapsed underneath themselves and cried together for so many reasons, shallow morals, mislaid friendships, and unrealized plans. They accepted that the dream was dead. The endless disappointments rocked them to the core, but the most disturbing realization of all was the inner knowledge that there was nothing more to do except go their separate ways.


19.


Nathan's final ounce of creativity was sucked out of him as he watched Nikki boarding a small commercial airliner out of Vanua Levu. Unable to breath, torrents of nostalgia crumbled into his defeated soul. He tried to think about the first night he met her, the earth-shattering circumstances that had brought them together, and the way they're relationship had matured through their journey. But a great wall of depression wound its way around the smoldering embers of his youth. He stopped her a last time and said, "I'll come back for you one day, you tell me when you're ready."

She was frantic as she asked, "Can we sing together again? Nothing ever made me feel more alive."

"Nikki, I hope we'll change the world together."

As she waved to him a last time through the window of the airport terminal, his emotions were in turmoil, freefalling away from the perfection of those times. Then he remembered how close he had been to finding the same freedom that Billy had found, wondering if he had made the right choice by hanging on. He sat alone waiting for the plane that would take him home, but it was hard as hell to be alive. With an empty life staring him in the face, reality was never so frightening.

Nikki slept though much of her short flight back to her parent's ranch in New Zealand. She had incessant dreams about a tiny speck of faith that was floating without direction in the limitless ocean. On the edge of her dreams, she could almost hear unremitting songs that were flowing with simplicity and genius. As her plane began its final decent, she woke up without a trace of memory regarding the nature of the dream. But years after her mind had given up on the fading wish, her heart did not cease to believe.

The changing world, so full of self-interest, misery, and degradation, had yet to experience such inspired elegance and unrestrained possibility. Drifting on the empty sea west of the Solomon Islands, a glimmer of movement bobbed past the setting sun. Alone in the calm water was a tiny yellow Zodiac that was battered beyond repair. Inside a worn chest strapped to the raft was a series of recordings that was one of the last great hopes for mankind. Years later, critics would ask how this music could possibly change the world. But Nikki knew his talent was a means to an end. She had seen something in Nathan's character that was extraordinary, while his ability to capture the human condition was remarkable. As she reflected on all that had happened, she came to believe that the successful release of his songs would give Nathan international recognition and professional opportunity. Only then could he do what he set out to do in this lifetime. And if the elusive gods of the universe were resolved to will those recordings into the right hands, then the hope, passion, and potential contained in his voice would one day lead a revolution to enrich cultures, ideas, and living beings across the planet.

## Epilogue

*Sunlight flashed in Nathan's eyes as he stepped off the airliner, making him squint as he searched the tarmac for signs of Nikki. Halfway down the stairs he noticed her silhouette sheathed in a stylish sundress waiting for him under a shady palm. She waved him over with controlled excitement; her body language spoke of maturity and contentment.*

*A spring of emotion rushed from his insides and he found himself running to her and then holding her with tender strength. For over a minute, words weren't needed to express the rising sentiment. Then Nathan looked her in the eyes and said, "My God I've missed you. I hope you know how much this means to me."*

*She smiled and nodded. He felt perfect in her arms, yet different somehow. His poise and decisiveness told her that he had* grown self-assured; he no longer needed other's approval for acceptance. Taking in the magnitude of the moment, she was sure that their separation had been worth it, the endless longing invaluable to their personal growth.

A touch of concern rolled from his lips as he asked, "So how are you?"

"I'm good. I really am. A bit nervous to see you, but very happy you came. How about we melt away together for a few days."

"There's nothing in this world that I'd rather do. But I need to know one thing. Of all the places on earth, why'd you ask me to meet you here?"

"Because I'm ready to face the memories with you, Luv. I want to take you to a place that's very special to me, where I learned how to cope with the pain of losing you the first time."

He was speechless, shaken by the power of her compassion. Nikki flagged down a rickshaw, and using hand gestures, directed the local to her sacred beach path. Slowly, they made their way to the end of the trail and sat on the water's edge. They pulled their knees to their chests and enjoyed the gentle waves lapping against their feet.

Secluded from the rest of the world, Nathan was able to explore her most intimate thoughts. He spoke with enthusiasm. "You've been gone so long. What've you been doing with yourself all this time?"

"Like I wrote in the letter, I've been traveling with the Peace Corps, keeping an eye on the lost children as they survive on this planet, trying to bring a little joy to their lives." Nikki was too modest to explain the extent to which she had become successful in her passions. She had gained local recognition in locations across the globe from her dedication to social work. And her creative talent was reflected by the fact that several of her photographs had won awards or appeared in magazines. A few months back she had taken a series of pictures of a Polynesian family working together with a fishing net at dusk and one of the prints had become a finalist for the International Photograph of the Year.

But instead of boasting about her accomplishments, she went in a more personal direction. "Really, what I've been doing is healing, learning as much as I can about the human race. I try to take in every moment, live every emotion. I might not be able to change the world, but I've come to terms with my issues and strengths, and try not to blame myself anymore."

"And how do you do that?"

"I guess if I had to narrow it down to one thing, I think it's that I've changed my lifestyle. Like I said to you at the end of our time together, I've been working on making better choices."

With that said, Nathan revealed a deeper level of his feelings. "Nikki, I tried to reach you several times early on. But I never heard back from you so I thought you'd moved on. That first year alone was an incredibly hard time in my life. I stayed on the path of destruction and hit bottom."

Nikki squeezed his hand, pained by his candor. "Nathan, I thought about you every day, but I don't think we could have made it. I don't regret our time on the ship, but I would've resented you had we stayed together back then. I had to get through my baggage;

232

*I needed to stop blaming myself for my sister's death and Billy's suicide before I could be right for you.   I didn't know if this time would ever come, but I always hoped."*

*"Thank you, I understand.  In fact, as hard as it is for me to admit, I think our time apart forced me to face my suffering.  Billy's death devastated me.  I still don't understand how everything unraveled."*

*It was Nikki's turn to pursue his hidden truths and she asked, "So what about you, how have you coped with what happened?"*

*"The first year was a spiral into hell, wandering around without direction or a plan.  But even at my lowest points, I realized I didn't want to end up like Billy; I had reason to live a healthy life. I began writing little notes to myself, reminders about you, my music, and how I wanted to treat people someday.   I knew I wanted to change, but didn't know how.   I realized I needed help but didn't know where to get it.  So I moved back to the California Coast, went back to college, and changed my major.  Psychology.  Can you believe it?   I cranked out four years of credits in two and got my degree.  Last month, I went home and made amends with Tamara and my parents.  But I couldn't stay long because I've just changed too much.  They still wanted to blame me for everything and I wouldn't let them.  But, at least I went and saw them, and I feel good about that."*

*Nikki was intrigued.  "I'm glad you feel comfortable enough to share all this.  I was hoping you were working on yourself while we were apart because it would have been harder to find out that you were still lost."*

*"Well, for a time there I was out of it. But, after I finally admitted my addiction to drinking and faced the grief I felt over the loss of you and Billy, things began making sense. I picked up surfing again and it became my healthy release because it allows me to get away and relax. Some of my psychology classes helped me understand the process of healing, but I got more out of studying on my own. I've done a lot of internal exploration and late night contemplation. I've kind of rebuilt myself from the inside. I don't know what I'm going to do with it, but I'm getting ready to face reality again."*

*Excitement was welling in her belly as she prepared to reveal her secret. "You mentioned your music. Are you still singing?"*

*He tried not to be guarded by the question. "Sometimes, when I'm alone. But I mostly keep it to myself. It's been hard to get back to that place again. I wish I wouldn't have lost all those recordings. It's still a big hole in my life."*

*She was teasing him now with her line of questioning. "You've come so far in so many ways. Well, what's next?" This penetrating question of hers always led to a prospect for change.*

*"Nikki, I might not have much right now, but I think I've learned a lot about the person I want to be. I'm twenty six years old and I'm ready to take a positive risk or two."*

*She could no longer contain her smile. "And do you see me as part of these risks you speak of?" Nikki beamed as she pulled a key chain from around her neck and placed it in his hands. She then removed the small chest from her backpack and placed it on the sand beside his feet.*

*"What's this?"*

*"It's my surprise. Just open it."*

*Nathan took the key and slowly removed the lock. Lifting the lid, he realized what was inside. A multitude of recordings stared up at him from the bottom of their dusty resting place. Joyous emotion overwhelmed him.*

*Nikki wiped a tear from her eye and said, "I've listened to them over and over again since that fisherman delivered them to my family. And they're even more incredible than I remember. You have many albums here, waiting for the right ears. They're raw but polished, familiar but different. I hope you understand that there's nothing else like them out there."*

*"Nikki, I don't know what to say."*

*"Don't say anything. Just tell me what you think of taking a holiday to California to get them produced?"*

*Nathan was quivering. "My God, it's all I've ever dreamed of doing."*

*He held out his hands and again held her in is arms, knowing that he had finally gotten it right. They sat there for some time watching the sun against the pale blue sky, ready to reach for a new direction.*

## ABOUT THE AUTHOR:

Jeff Kozlowski is a graduate of Central Michigan University where he received a Bachelors degree in Special Education and History. He is currently obtaining his Masters Degree from California State University San Marcos in School Administration. He works as the Director of Education at a private school in Del Mar that challenges students with unique learning strategies.

Jeff has always utilized writing as a way to reach future generations and weaves his own personal life lessons into his stories. He has written two fiction novels titled *Fronters Gaining the Flow* and *The One*. He has also published numerous short stories, articles and poems on the human condition.

Jeff Kozlowski currently lives in San Diego with his wife and two children.

---

To contact Jeff about his works or
for more information about his writing,
please visit the following websites.

www.myspace.com/jeffkozlowski
www.jeffkozlowski.blogspot.com
www.lulu.com/jeffkozlowski

If you have any questions or comments,
please fee free to email Jeff at:

jeffreykozlowski@yahoo.com

---